The Mystery
of the Haunted
Playhouse

Laura E. Williams

SCHOLASTIC INC.

New York Toronto London Auckland Sydney
Mexico City New Delhi Hong Kong Buenos Aires

For the Till family

A Roundtable Press Book

For Roundtable Press, Inc.:
Directors: Julie Merberg, Marsha Melnick, Susan E. Meyer
Project Editor: Meredith Wolf Schizer
Editorial Assistant: Sara Newberry
Designer: Elissa Stein
Illustrator: Laura Hartman Maestro

ISBN 0-439-21730-X

12 11 10 9 8 7 6 5 4 3 2   2 3 4 5 6/0

Printed in the U.S.A.
First Scholastic printing, December 2001

Contents

	Note to Reader	v
1	The Werewolf in the Woods	1
2	The Auditions	8
3	Lights Out	15
4	A Strange Sound	27
5	The Death Threat	35
6	After Hours	43
7	A Falling Star	52
8	Mistaken Identity	62
9	The Search	69
10	A Perfect Match	79
11	What's Next?	87
12	Knocked Out!	94
	Note to Reader	107
	Solution—Another Mystery Solved!	108

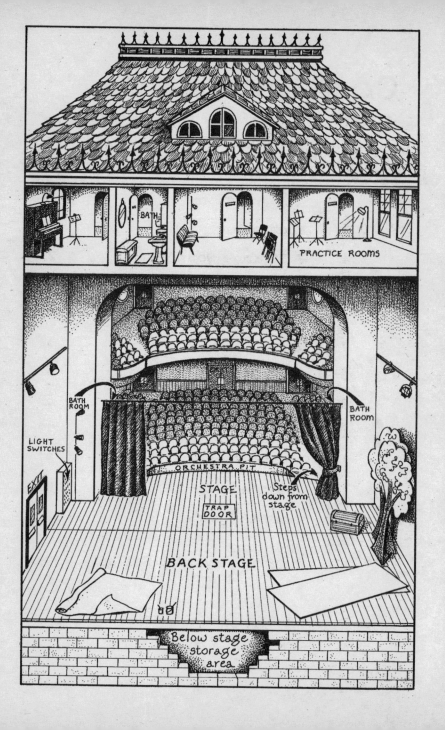

BATH

PRACTICE ROOMS

BATH
ROOM

BATH
ROOM

LIGHT
SWITCHES

EXIT

ORCHESTRA PIT

STAGE

Steps
down from
stage

TRAP
DOOR

BACK STAGE

Below stage
storage
area

Note to Reader

Welcome to *The Mystery of the Haunted Playhouse*, where YOU solve the mystery. As you read, look for clues pointing to the guilty person. There is a blank suspect sheet in the back of this book. You can copy it to keep track of the clues you find throughout the story. It is the same as the suspect sheets that Jen and Zeke will use later in the story when they try to solve the mystery. Can you solve *The Mystery of the Haunted Playhouse* before they do?

Good luck!

The Werewolf in the Woods

Zeke looked up at the Mystic Playhouse, a tall, narrow building that sat on a small grassy hill in the distance. "It looks like the house in Alfred Hitchcock's movie *Psycho*," he said, lowering his voice to make it sound spooky.

Jen shivered beside her twin brother. "Creepy," she whispered. The old playhouse had been reno-vated recently, but in spite of the fresh paint, it still had a haunted look to it.

As if reading her mind, Zeke asked, "Did you hear about the ghost?"

"Is this one of your lame jokes?" Jen asked, glancing sideways at her brother. The Maine wind whipped his wavy brown hair around his face.

"It's not a joke. One of the workmen said he heard a really strange moaning sound in the playhouse one

1

night," Zeke answered, his blue eyes sparkling.

Jen hunched her shoulders, trying to keep the cold off her neck. "It was probably just the wind blowing through the old place."

Zeke shrugged. "Probably," he agreed. He started off ahead of Jen. "Come on, or we'll be late."

They hustled up the last part of the hill and entered the playhouse through the red side door. A sign above it read CAST AND CREW. The playhouse was already filling up with chatty kids from the middle school and the local high school, arriving for the upcoming musical tryouts.

Just inside the door, Jen and Zeke noticed Joe and Alice Pinelli, the new owners of the theater. They were whispering as they stood off to the side of the room, near the big green box that held the light switches for the entire theater. Joe, a tall, thin man with straight posture, white hair, and a gray-and-white mustache, gave them a halfhearted smile. Alice, his wife, who kept her white hair pulled into a large bun at the nape of her neck, was holding her head like she had a terrible headache.

"Hi," Jen said to them, wondering why the couple looked so upset. "Is everything okay?"

Alice lowered her hands and relaxed her face into a slight smile, but the smile didn't extend to her pale green eyes. She still looked distracted, and she didn't answer Jen.

Joe shook his head. "We're not too pleased about this musical," he said, his voice low and gruff.

"You mean *The Werewolf in the Woods?*" Zeke asked.

"Right," said Alice, frowning. "I mean, we're not quite done renovating the theater."

"I thought you said everything was finished," Zeke said.

Alice waved her hands vaguely in the air. "Well . . . everything big may be finished, but there are still a lot of small details to attend to."

Jen looked around. "It looks great to me. What else needs to be done?"

Joe scowled down at her. "There are a lot of things. I don't like rushing. Rush, rush, rush, just to perform the play by a certain date. Ridiculous!"

"But it's so exciting," Jen said, trying to cheer up the older couple. The Pinellis were friends of the twins' aunt Bee, and they'd recently moved to Mystic to take over management of the playhouse. Joe's father had owned and run it for many years. He had finally retired, and Joe had taken over. Just last week he and Alice had been so excited about all the renovations they were doing in the old building, including new curtains, newly upholstered chairs, and a modern catwalk, among other things. Now what was wrong?

"Don't you think it's exciting?" Zeke pressed, wondering why the Pinellis were acting so weird. "We're going to perform *The Werewolf in the Woods* on the exact fiftieth anniversary of its very first performance here."

Joe and Alice glanced at each other but made no comment about whether the show was exciting or not. Joe just muttered under his breath, "Rush, rush, rush."

"We'd better get in there," Zeke said, pulling on Jen's arm. He didn't want to be late for the tryouts. They said good-bye to the Pinellis and headed toward the side stage area.

"I wonder what's *really* wrong with the Pinellis," Jen whispered to Zeke when they'd descended the side steps off the stage and were settling into seats right in front of the empty orchestra pit.

"How can they not be excited about *The Werewolf in the Woods?*" Zeke wondered. "I'm hoping to get a part as one of the victims. I'll get to die a gory death. Just think of all that great fake blood I'll get to use."

"You're sick," Jen said with a grin. She tucked a strand of brown hair behind her ear. "But seriously, why wouldn't the Pinellis be happy about this show? This is the musical that made Alaina Shine famous."

"Right," Zeke agreed, "and tons of people will come to see this revival, since it's opening on the show's anniversary, when Alaina was discovered by a Hollywood talent scout. The Pinellis will rake in the dough on this one. It'll probably pay for all their renovations."

"So why did Mrs. Pinelli look so mad?"

Zeke shrugged. "How should I know what's going on with them?"

"I'm going to ask Aunt Bee," Jen proclaimed.

The twins had lived with their aunt Bee since their parents were killed in a car accident when they were two years old. Aunt Bee ran the local Mystic Lighthouse Bed and Breakfast—with their help, of course. The B&B was such a success, it always kept her very busy. Unfortunately, Uncle Cliff had died two years ago, right before the B&B's grand opening. But Aunt Bee had the twins to help her, as well as Detective Wilson and other good friends like the Pinellis. Aunt Bee would know for sure what was wrong with Joe and Alice.

Jen's best friend, Stacey, plopped into the seat next to Jen. "It's pretty cool-looking in here," she said, tipping her head back to stare at the high ceiling that was painted with clouds and stars and gold cherubs in each corner.

"Are you trying out for a part?" Jen asked, surprised to see her best friend at the auditions.

"No way," she said, shaking her blond curls. "I can't sing to save my life." She pulled out her reporter's notebook. "I'm here to write a story about the musical and the mysterious Alaina Shine: hometown girl, Hollywood legend."

Jen laughed. "That sounds like the title of an article."

"It is," Stacey said, her light blue eyes shining. "Do you like it?"

"Alaina Shine: Hometown Girl, Hollywood Legend," Jen repeated. "Sounds good to me!"

Stacey clicked her pen, poised to write. "So, what's the musical about?"

Zeke leaned over Jen and said, "Nothing like doing your research ahead of time."

"Hey, what do you think I'm doing now?" Stacey retorted. Then she looked at Jen again. "Well?"

"*The Werewolf in the Woods* is about a girl werewolf," Jen began, talking slowly so Stacey could take notes. "This werewolf girl is really sweet, but on nights when there's a full moon, she prowls the forests as a werewolf and kills anyone she comes across."

"Gross!" Stacey exclaimed, but she didn't stop writing.

Zeke leaned across again. "She's going to kill me," he said, grinning at the girls.

"Good," Stacey said.

Jen laughed at the frown on her brother's face. "Anyway, the werewolf girl rallies the town into organizing a hunt for this monster, knowing that it'll mean her own death. In the end, she sings this beautiful song just as a hunter's arrow pierces her heart and she dies."

"How depressing," Stacey said after she'd snapped her notebook closed.

"It's that last song that made Alaina Shine famous," Jen pointed out. "The Hollywood talent scout was amazed by her performance and whisked her off to California, where she made fourteen movies in seven years."

Zeke leaned over his sister one last time. He lowered his voice to a dramatic growl. "And then she disappeared forever!"

The Auditions

Stacey visibly shuddered. "What a bummer!"

Jen nodded. "More than a bummer," she said. "Tragic. Imagine being that famous and glamorous, and then dying at the height of your fame."

"And it happened right here in Mystic," Zeke added. "She went out for a sail, a storm blew in, and she was never seen again. In fact—"

"Attention!" someone shouted. Immediately, the entire theater became silent. Everyone recognized the brash voice of Mr. Hague, the director.

Jen ducked down in her seat. She knew from rumors that it was best not to be singled out by Mr. Hague. He had wild black hair that frizzed around his tan face. With every word, he threw his hands through the air, gesturing wildly with his baton or with the musical score rolled up like a club.

"If you would all please shut your mouths, we can get started!" he shouted.

"I absolutely agree," sang out a high voice.

Zeke couldn't believe someone had interrupted Mr. Hague. He turned to watch a rather stout woman barreling down the aisle from the rear of the theater. Behind her trailed a girl with long, shiny black hair and downcast eyes: Kate Kizme. Zeke recognized her even though she was a freshman at the high school.

Mrs. Kizme didn't stop till she was practically nose to nose with Mr. Hague. "Now that Kate is here, you may begin," she said.

"How wonderful for us," Mr. Hague said, clearly sarcastic. Mrs. Kizme didn't seem to notice.

"That's right, dear," she said, pulling her daughter closer. "You will try out first. After all, once you've tried out, it'll be obvious who should play Alaina Shine's part!"

"I am the director," Mr. Hague said through clenched teeth. "I make the decisions. I say who tries out first, second, third—and who doesn't try out at all!"

"Clearly my Kate should audition first," Mrs. Kizme argued, much to everyone's astonishment. No one ever argued with Mr. Hague. "It will save you a lot of time with the rest of the tryouts if everyone knows you've already chosen the star." She patted her daughter lightly on the shoulder.

Kate didn't lift her head. Her dark hair draped like curtains down either side of her face. Jen squirmed with embarrassment for the older girl.

"Very well," Mr. Hague said, still clenching his teeth. "Kate, get on stage and sing your prepared piece."

Mrs. Kizme clapped her ringed fingers together. "Go on, dear," she urged, nudging Kate forward.

No one spoke as the girl climbed the side steps onto the stage. Standing stage center, she waited until her mother had given the piano player her piece. At a nod from the pianist, she opened her mouth.

Zeke stared in amazement as Kate sang. Her voice came out first like soft, shimmering silk. But by the climax of the song, her words burst out loud and clear and ringing with strength. His skin prickled with goose bumps. As the last note died away, the audience sat silent, then everyone burst into applause.

Kate didn't even smile. She simply shrugged and headed offstage to join her mother, who was glowing with pleasure.

"You see?" Mrs. Kizme called to Mr. Hague. "You have your star!"

"Next," Mr. Hague bellowed, ignoring Mrs. Kizme's comment.

Zeke whispered to Jen, "He'll have to choose her.

She's got an awesome voice."

"True, but I don't think Mr. Hague likes to be told what to do," Jen whispered back.

Tommy slid into the seat next to Zeke. "I'm not trying out," he said quickly, before Zeke could ask what his best friend was doing there. "No way am I singing onstage for a bunch of strangers. I'm here to help paint scenery. Jen said I had to."

Jen smiled at him and he pretended to scowl. She already knew she'd be part of the crew—there was always a shortage of behind-the-scenes workers—and she'd asked Tommy and Stacey to join her.

Several girls tried out for the leading part, but no one had a voice to equal Kate's. The boys tried out for the lead male part of the hunter, and then the smaller roles auditioned. Finally, it was Zeke's turn.

"What part do you hope to get?" Mr. Hague asked, brushing his fingers through his wild hair.

"I want to die a horrible death," Zeke declared.

"Can you sing at the same time?"

To prove it, Zeke sang one of the chorus parts from *The Werewolf in the Woods* and managed to writhe in pain at the same time until he fell down on the stage, quite dead. The audience cheered and hooted, and Tommy pierced the air with a long whistle.

"Hey, maybe I *should* try out for this thing,"

Tommy said, still clapping for Zeke. "I didn't know there'd be cool stuff like that in it."

Jen rolled her eyes. "You still have to sing, you know. It's not just being devoured by a cute werewolf."

"Oh," Tommy said. "Right." He shrugged. "Anyway, you need me to help paint scenery."

Suddenly a teenage girl ran onto the stage, completely out of breath. "I'm sorry," she cried. "I'm sorry I'm late, Mr. Hague. My mom's car broke down and I had to run here and —"

Zeke looked at the girl who had just dashed into the spotlight. He got up from his death fall and returned to his seat.

"Heather Elliot," Mr. Hague said brusquely, "we've already had auditions for the werewolf part."

"But it wasn't my fault," Heather wailed. She had sandy-blond hair that curled up at her shoulders; it was held back by a red band. "Please let me audition!"

Mr. Hague stomped his foot, his hands clenched into fists at his side. "I do not do favors for anyone, Miss Elliot. You should know that by now!"

"You're absolutely right," Mrs. Kizme interjected from the front row. "She was late, and that's that."

Mr. Hague whipped around and shot Mrs. Kizme a dark look. "On second thought," he said, turning back to face Heather, "you may audition."

Mrs. Kizme gasped with fury and Heather grinned. She threw her windbreaker into the wings. After clearing her throat, she belted out a song.

"She sounds great," Jen said to Zeke.

He nodded. "Her voice is strong, but she doesn't have as much range as Kate."

Jen shrugged. It sounded good to her. But what did she know about singing? She could kick a soccer ball right where she aimed it, but forget about hitting any particular musical note. She either ended up too high or too low, and everyone around her always winced when she sang. She took that as a clue to stick to soccer and leave the singing to Zeke and people like Heather and Kate.

When Heather finished she gave a fancy little bow while everyone clapped enthusiastically for her. Everyone except Mrs. Kizme, Zeke noticed.

"Good job," Mr. Hague said, smiling for once.

Heather beamed and bounced off the stage.

"She can be the werewolf's sister," Mrs. Kizme said in a loud voice, rushing over to the director. "My Kate is still the very best for the leading role."

"*I* am the director," Mr. Hague responded sharply. "*I* will make the final decision."

"But even an idiot can see that Kate is far better." Mrs. Kizme turned to Heather. "No offense, dear, but you were late and you missed Kate's audition. It was quite spectacular."

Heather stared at her with an open mouth while Kate slipped deeper and deeper into her seat, looking down at the floor so that her hair covered most of her reddened face. Mr. Hague looked like he was going to leap off the stage and strangle Mrs. Kizme.

Realizing that she may have pushed him too far, Mrs. Kizme quieted down. "Did I tell you that I'm calling talent scouts from Hollywood and Broadway to attend on opening night?" she asked in a new, sweet voice. "Perhaps a scout will discover the brilliant director!"

Mr. Hague's mouth snapped closed with an audible click.

"I can tell that the idea appeals to you," Mrs. Kizme said slyly. "All you have to do is cast Kate in the role she was born for, and who knows what might happen to your career!"

Without another word, Mr. Hague gathered up his notes and stuffed them into a large bag he'd brought with him. "Broadway," he muttered, so that only those sitting close to the front could hear him.

Jen and Zeke glanced at each other. Would Mr. Hague cast Kate as the werewolf just for a shot at Broadway? Could he be longing for stardom himself?

3

Lights Out

Late Sunday morning at the B&B, Zeke stuffed half a fluffy pancake into his mouth. "Mmmm," he said after he'd swallowed. "These are the best pancakes in the world."

Jen skidded into the kitchen. Woofer, their Old English sheepdog, and Slinky, their Maine coon cat, trotted along close at her heels.

She looked around. "Did I miss brunch?"

Aunt Bee turned from the stove. She wore a long flower-printed skirt, as she usually did, with a turquoise top. Her long gray hair was neatly braided down her back. "Zeke is trying to eat all the pancakes," she said, "but I managed to save a bit of the batter for you."

Jen plunked herself down at the small kitchen table where they ate when there were no others to feed. "No guests this morning?" she asked, wondering why the B&B was so quiet.

Aunt Bee waved her yellow spatula. "Are you kidding? You slept through the brunch I made for the Reynolds' family reunion. You must have been up late watching television."

"Actually, I was reading a mystery. I couldn't put it down until I found out who had stolen the golden apple." She yawned. "I really hate it when books are that good."

Aunt Bee and Zeke laughed. They knew how much Jen loved a good book.

"Anyway," Aunt Bee continued, "the rest of the rooms are empty right now. But I did get several calls from reporters who want to book rooms for the upcoming show."

"Already?" Zeke said. "That was quick."

"Mrs. Kizme must be getting out the word just like she said she would," Jen commented after she took a gulp of the freshly squeezed orange juice Aunt Bee had prepared earlier.

"Are any talent scouts staying here?" Zeke asked hopefully.

Jen laughed. "Why? Do you want to be discovered as the greatest dying boy of all time?"

Zeke grinned. "You have to admit, my death

spasms were pretty awesome."

Aunt Bee chuckled as she placed a plate of pancakes in front of Jen. "I'm sorry to disappoint you, but no talent scouts have called. One reporter is coming in today, though. He said he's with some big city paper." She sat at the table with the twins and frowned.

Jen glanced at her aunt, who was usually so cheerful. She wondered why Aunt Bee suddenly looked so glum.

Zeke noticed the change in their aunt, too. "What's wrong?"

"Oh, all this to-do about the revival of *The Werewolf in the Woods*. Why can't they just leave poor Alaina Shine's memory to rest in peace?"

Jen and Zeke looked at each other. They had twin telepathy and Zeke knew his sister wanted him to keep his mouth shut, but he couldn't help saying, "Do you really think she's dead?"

For a moment, Aunt Bee stared off into space. "I suppose so," she said slowly. "But now all her fans, old and new, will come to Mystic again and try to dig up the truth about her disappearance. It was quite shocking forty-three years ago when she vanished in the storm. They say she wasn't too far out in the bay, yet the boat and her body were never found."

"I wonder if it had anything to do with Poseidon's Triangle," Jen said, thinking of the strange patch of ocean just off the coast where legend had it that sea serpents had been spotted and boats sank for no reason.

"The police finally called it an accidental drowning, right?" Zeke prodded.

Aunt Bee nodded.

"What was she like as a kid?" Jen asked gently. She knew Alaina Shine and Aunt Bee had been classmates and good friends before Alaina had been "discovered." "You don't have to answer if it's too painful," Jen added hastily.

"Heavens no," Aunt Bee said with a wave of her hand. "We were friends over fifty years ago. Once she went off to Hollywood, she was so busy I hardly ever heard from her. But when we were classmates, we were the best of friends. She was quiet and sweet and a rather private person. I think all the stardom and attention the world heaped on Alaina was very difficult for her to bear. She had to leave all her friends and family back here. I think she was terribly lonely in Hollywood."

Silence settled on the bright kitchen filled with bee decorations. Jen couldn't imagine being pulled out of Mystic, where practically everyone knew one another, only to be shoved into a life of glamorous parties and strangers all around. Jen had always thought it would be fun to be famous, but suddenly it seemed rather sad.

She ate another forkful of pancakes dripping with syrup. With his nose, Woofer nudged her elbow hopefully, and she couldn't help laughing, breaking the solemn silence.

"Yes, you can lick my plate," she promised the huge dog. "But don't rush me."

"Hello," said a voice from the kitchen doorway. All three of them jumped in their seats.

Aunt Bee pressed a hand to her heart. "My goodness, you startled us," she said, standing up.

A stranger entered the kitchen, smiling sheepishly. He stood at medium height, with brown hair and bottle-green eyes, and wore a casual sweater and dark, pressed jeans. "Sorry about that," he said quickly. "I arrived early and didn't see anyone at the front desk, so I came looking for you. I followed my nose," he said appreciatively, eyeing the empty plate Jen was just putting on the floor for Woofer.

"You must be Larry Tomkins," Aunt Bee said. "The reporter."

"That's right," the man said with a smile. "But I'm really more of a theater critic than a reporter."

"What paper do you work for?" Zeke asked, wondering why he hadn't heard the man approaching before he startled them all at the door.

"The *New York Times*," he mumbled. "Is there any way I can get something to eat?" he asked.

"B&B," Aunt Bee said, "stands for bed and breakfast, or in this case brunch, so if you don't mind eating in the kitchen, sit down and I'll whip up another batch of pancakes."

Larry sat down. "Great," he said.

"We have to get to the Mystic Playhouse pretty soon," Zeke said, standing up. "Mr. Hague is posting the cast list today. Can you give us a ride, Aunt Bee?"

Before she could answer, Larry said, "I was planning on heading over there myself. If you can wait until I eat, I'll be happy to give you a ride there — and a ride home, too. I plan on staying through the entire rehearsal."

Since that seemed like the best solution for everyone, and Larry insisted he didn't mind, Jen and Zeke went to their rooms to collect their things. Before his death, Uncle Cliff had renovated the old lighthouse tower so that Zeke and Jen each had a round bedroom with views out to the harbor and the Atlantic Ocean. A few minutes later they met in the foyer to wait for Larry.

"Did you hear him come in?" Jen asked in a low

voice, not wanting to be overheard. While she could always count on her sharp eyesight, her brother's hearing was ten times better than hers.

He shook his head, frowning. "I was just as surprised to see him standing there as you and Aunt Bee. He walks more quietly than anyone I know, like his feet don't even touch the ground. He must practice it or something."

"Ready to go?" Larry asked, practically right behind them.

Jen yelped with surprise as both twins whirled around. She glanced down at Larry's brown leather shoes. They didn't look any quieter than normal shoes, but he sure had a way of sneaking up on people without being heard.

He smiled at the twins. "Did I startle you?"

Zeke shook his head. "Nah, we heard you coming a mile away."

Jen rolled her eyes at her brother and he grinned back at her.

At the theater, a number of students crowded around the side door. Mr. Hague would be there any moment to post the cast list on the bulletin board. Too nervous to wait patiently inside, everyone milled around outside, waiting for Mr. Hague to arrive. Jen and Zeke joined the group, with Larry not far behind them.

"Don't worry," Jen said in Zeke's ear. "You'll definitely get a dying part. No one died as well as you."

Zeke smiled at her. "Thanks, sis."

Someone tapped Jen on the arm, and she was surprised to find Kate Kizme standing beside her. Kate kept her head lowered as though she didn't want anyone to recognize her.

"Hey, you're in charge of scenery, right?" Kate asked.

"Well, sort of," Jen replied. She'd had more experience than the other kids helping out backstage and would probably wind up in charge.

"Look, if you need any help designing sets or painting or even sewing costumes, let me know, okay? I'd love to help out."

"Uh, yeah, sure," Jen stammered. But, she wanted to ask, wouldn't Kate be too busy to help backstage if she got the starring role?

"Katie, dear," Mrs. Kizme called, pushing through the crowd. "There you are. I was looking all over for you. Mr. Hague is just getting out of his car!" The woman barely gave Jen a glance, then swept her daughter off with her.

Jen shrugged. She was only the backstage help. No talent scout was going to "discover" her, which was just fine. Especially if stardom meant having to deal with people like Mrs. Kizme!

As Mr. Hague approached, the crowd separated, giving him a clear path to the stage door. He didn't look right or left, but walked as if he were a king among his subjects. Like everyone else, Zeke longed to pounce on the sheet of paper he saw clutched in the director's hand. He had no choice but to wait patiently while Mr. Hague entered the theater, everyone crowding in behind him, and tacked up the list. As soon as he left, the hopefuls surged forward, crushing anyone in the front of the crowd.

"Yes!" Zeke cheered, seeing his name listed as *werewolf's third victim*. "I get to die onstage!"

A sudden screech pierced the air.

"Eeeee, Katie! You're the star! I just knew that awful man would see things my way! Eeeee! Eeeee!" Mrs. Kizme squealed.

Someone shoved against Zeke. Heather Elliot, her face dark with fury, stormed by.

"Come on, Zeke," Jen said, grabbing his arm. "Let's go say hi to the Pinellis."

The older couple had been watching everything from beside one of the stage curtains. They didn't look any happier today than they had yesterday. Jen wished she had remembered to ask Aunt Bee what was bothering them.

Since Larry was still with them, Jen introduced him to Joe and Alice. "Larry Tomkins is a theater critic."

Larry smiled broadly and offered his hand. "How do you do?"

"Fine," Joe said as he shook the hand briefly before letting it go. Alice didn't say anything, but kept her lips pressed together so tightly a white ring formed around them.

"Could I ask you some questions about this old theater?" Larry asked, pulling out a small black tape recorder like the one Jen had received for a birthday present the year before.

"Not now," Joe said brusquely. Without saying good-bye, he ushered his wife away from them.

Larry watched them go and shrugged. "I'll get my answers later," he told the twins. "I always do."

"We'd better introduce you to the director," Zeke said, not sure how Mr. Hague would respond to having a newspaperman in the audience before they'd even been able to rehearse.

They led Larry over to the director, who was already yelling at one of the older boys. "Get it right or get out!" Mr. Hague finished. Then he spun toward them, a frown making his dark eyes look even darker.

"Uh, this is Larry Tomkins, a reporter," Zeke said

quickly, wanting to get the introduction over with as soon as possible.

"What a complete pleasure to meet you, Mr. Tomkins," Mr. Hague gushed, with a little bob. In fact, it was almost a bow.

Zeke stared at the director in amazement. He'd expected Mr. Hague to throw Larry out or at least throw something at him. But what did he know about moody directors?

"I'm sure I've read your reviews many times," Mr. Hague went on. "How wonderful that you can join us. Of course, please remember this will be the first readthrough, but I'm sure you'll be entertained."

"I'm sure I will be," Larry agreed.

Zeke couldn't believe these smooth words were coming out of Mr. Hague's mouth. As Larry settled into the third row of seats, Zeke ran off to collect his script, and Jen joined her group of backstage workers. Stacey and Tommy showed up as they'd promised.

Mr. Hague demanded quiet, then he had the actors read through the script. Jen became so involved in her own work, she barely noticed what was happening onstage. But when the musical reached the climactic scene where Kate had been pierced by an arrow and was singing her dying song to the full moon, everyone stopped what they were doing to watch and listen. Mr. Hague didn't stop her once to correct anything.

Kate's voice rose and fell, almost like a lonely howl, as she sang about how sad she was to go but how much safer the village would be now. Shivers raced up and down Jen's back. She glanced out into the darkened audience, but her sharp eyes couldn't find Larry in his seat.

In a last high note, Kate's werewolf character died with her arms stretched up to the moon. Just at that chilling moment, all the lights in the theater blinked out!

4

A Strange Sound

Panicked voices shouted, "Turn on the lights!"

"Hey, what's going on?"

"Ouch!"

"Don't move, anyone!"

"Katie, dear, where are you? I'm coming to find you. Don't panic."

"Please," Joe Pinelli's voice rose above the hubbub, "don't anyone move. I'll get the lights back on straight away."

Jen stood stock-still. She didn't relish the idea of banging her shins on anything or bashing into anyone. With a room full of actors, it seemed like they all had to act, in her opinion. More like *over*act. What was a little darkness anyway?

A minute later, the lights blazed back to life. Everyone cheered. Joe Pinelli didn't look pleased when he said, "I told you this theater isn't ready for a show. This old wiring system can't take the strain."

Jen frowned.

"Why the funny face?" Stacey asked.

"She was born with it," Tommy joked, joining the two of them.

"Ha. Very ha," Stacey retorted, jabbing him in the ribs. She turned to Jen again, waiting for an answer.

"It's just what Joe Pinelli said about the theater's electrical system. All the wires were replaced over a month ago."

"Are you sure?" Stacey asked.

Jen nodded. "I remember the Pinellis telling Aunt Bee about it because it was such a big, expensive job. There's nothing wrong with the lighting system. I'm sure of it."

Tommy leaned forward and in a stage whisper said, "Maybe the rumors about Alaina Shine are true! Maybe her ghost turned off the lights!"

"Why would she do that?" Stacey said.

Tommy shrugged. "She's not happy about this revival of *The Werewolf in the Woods*? In a way, it's this musical that led to her death."

"Or maybe she's jealous that someone else is playing the role that made her famous," Stacey mused.

"It was never proved that she's actually dead," Jen pointed out.

"You three!" Mr. Hague shouted at them. "Get off my stage! How can I run a rehearsal with you standing there like bumps on a log? If you can't find something constructive to do, get out!"

Jen felt her face flush as she hustled out of the way. She nearly ran into her brother, who was standing just offstage.

Zeke patted her on the shoulder. "Don't feel bad; he yells at everyone. Half the town hates him. Of course, the other half loves him because he produces awesome shows. So just forget about it."

"I'll try," Jen mumbled as she hurried away. She didn't want to get yelled at again for standing around.

For the next few hours, Jen was so busy backstage organizing props, making a list of scenery they would need, and trying to figure out which pulleys pulled which backdrops, she practically forgot about the harsh scolding. Around dinnertime everyone took a break and split up into groups to devour the pizza that had been delivered.

"Mmmm," Tommy said, his mouth stuffed with food. "Greath pitha!"

Zeke knew it was hopeless trying to teach Tommy

any manners. When it came to eating, Tommy forgot everything he'd been taught. All he cared about was getting the food into his mouth and enjoying it. Zeke stuffed another bite into his own mouth, grinning to himself. The pizza *was* great. Maybe that's why he and Tommy were best friends — they both liked good food.

The four friends sat in a circle at the edge of the stage with Larry Tomkins. Zeke had invited the reporter to join them.

"How do you like the show so far?" Zeke asked the reporter.

Larry nodded. "You are all doing a super job. That Kate Kizme has a beautiful voice."

"So does Heather Elliot," Jen said.

"Heather is Kate's understudy," Zeke said, helping himself to another slice of pepperoni pizza. "So unless Kate gets laryngitis or breaks her leg on opening night, Heather's out of luck."

"Did you see the look on her face when Mr. Hague posted the list?" Jen added.

Zeke nodded. "She was totally furious."

"If looks could kill!" Jen said.

"So how do you like being a reporter?" Stacey asked Larry, changing the subject.

Jen caught a flash of bitterness cross Larry's face

before he smiled. Or had she imagined it?

"It's great," Larry said, looking at the two leftover slices of pizza as if deciding whether or not to take another piece. "Very competitive, though, unless you bring in a cutting-edge story."

"That's what I'm going to do," Stacey informed them. She lowered her voice. "I'm going to find out what really happened to Alaina Shine. I'm going to solve the mystery!"

Larry chuckled. "If someone did break that story, it would be *huge* news and worth enormous amounts of money in articles, interviews — even a book contract. But," he added, holding up his hands as if to stop traffic, "reporters and fans have been trying to solve that mystery for forty-three years, and no one has come up with a single clue. Not even the police."

"Just because the police can't figure out something doesn't mean that Jen and Zeke can't solve it," Stacey said, lifting her chin defiantly. "They've solved lots of mysteries, and they're going to help me solve this one, too."

"We are?" Zeke said.

Stacey gave him a dark look. He got the hint and stuffed another bite of pizza into his mouth.

"Good luck," said Larry sarcastically.

"So," Jen cut in, "you like the show. That's great."

"Kept me glued to my seat. I never left," Larry said, nodding.

"Really? But—"

Mr. Hague clapped his hands. Everyone jumped up. No one wanted to get yelled at, especially Jen. She gathered the pizza box and empty plastic cups and hustled to the trash before getting back to work. Even Larry seemed to want to get out of the way. He hurried back to his seat. Jen pursed her lips. Had the reporter been glued to his seat the whole time? Then why hadn't she seen him out there when she'd specifically been looking for him?

With a shrug, she focused on organizing all of the plywood trees for the forest scene. There was way too much work to do to waste time wondering where Larry spent every second.

By nine o'clock, everyone was pretty well exhausted. Even Mrs. Kizme, who had been arguing with Mr. Hague about blocking and every little thing that had to do with Kate, had quieted down and now sat in the audience beside Larry.

"She's probably trying to get him to write an exclusive article about Kate," Zeke whispered in Jen's ear.

Jen nodded, too tired to answer.

"I'll see you all after school tomorrow," Mr. Hague said. "Don't be late."

The theater emptied out quickly until only Jen, Zeke, and Larry were left, with a single stage light burning.

"Aren't you ready yet?" Zeke moaned. "Do you always have to be the last one?"

"Sorry," Jen said, "but I want to have everything in order for tomorrow's rehearsal. There's so much to do in the next two and a half weeks," she grumbled. "I'm beginning to think the Pinellis are right and we're rushing this show too much."

"Hurry up, will you?" Zeke said, tapping his foot. Something about the old theater gave him the creeps — not that he'd admit it to anyone. Now that the rest of the group had left, the stage felt lonely and very spooky with just a dim light on.

"Okay, I'm done," Jen said, ten minutes later. "We can go."

Even Larry looked tired as he led them out to his car. Tired from what? Zeke wondered. Sitting around all day?

"Rats," Jen exclaimed as she was about to buckle her seat belt. "I forgot my notes. If they get lost, I'm dead." Before anyone could stop her, she jumped out of the car and raced to the side door of the theater. She remembered exactly where she'd left them, but she was sure if she didn't take them now, someone would move them by tomorrow.

Jen pulled the door open and hurried to the back-stage area. A few lights were left on twenty-four hours a day, so she didn't trip over anything.

Even in sneakers, her footsteps echoed eerily in the empty theater. She grabbed her papers, resisting the urge to run out of there.

Suddenly, a sound caught her attention. She froze, the hair on the back of her neck prickling. A ghostly moaning filled the air!

5

The Death Threat

Jen took a deep breath to steady her suddenly jumpy nerves. She walked carefully but quickly through the tables and boxes and clothes racks backstage to get to the side door.

The moaning continued, wavering and flowing like water as it became louder and then softer and then louder again. *It couldn't be Alaina Shine's ghost, could it?* That thought made her pick up her speed. She knocked her shin against a toolbox. With a loud cry of pain, Jen tried to massage her throbbing shin and hop out of there at the same time.

The eerie sound trailed off. A heavy dark silence settled in the theater, which was somehow even more dreadful than the spooky moaning.

Wincing with each step, Jen ran the last few feet out of the building. She didn't stop till she got to the car.

"What's wrong?" Zeke exclaimed when she yanked the car door closed behind her.

Jen took a deep breath and massaged her sore shin. "N-nothing," she gasped, realizing she must have been holding her breath in the theater because suddenly breathing felt so good. "I just tripped over something."

Larry eyed her in the rearview mirror. "You sure?" he asked.

"Yes," she insisted.

Zeke, also in the front seat, turned around to look at her more carefully. She gave him a warning look, hoping he'd just leave it alone for now. Sure enough, he got her mental message and didn't ask any more questions until they were home and alone in Jen's bedroom.

"So what really happened?" Zeke asked, flopping onto her blow-up chair and tossing aside a sweatshirt Jen hadn't bothered to fold and put away.

Jen sat on the edge of her bed and shivered. "I heard the spookiest sound in the theater."

"The munching of little mouse teeth?" Zeke teased.

"No, I'm serious. It was like a weird moaning or groaning sound."

Zeke sat up a little straighter. "Like a ghost?"

Jen shrugged one shoulder. "I don't know. I've never heard a real ghost before. But whatever it was, it gave me the creeps."

"It was probably just the wind blowing through the creaky old building, like you said before."

"But there isn't any wind tonight." Jen pointed at the calm bay outside her bedroom window.

Zeke frowned. "Oh, right."

"Why couldn't it be Alaina Shine's ghost?"

"I thought you didn't believe in ghosts," Zeke said.

Jen threw up her hands. "What else could it be? It wasn't the wind, no one else was on the stage. . . ." she trailed off. It was true that she didn't believe in ghosts, but she couldn't explain the sound, either.

Zeke stood up and yawned. "I'm going to bed. Mr. Hague sure makes us work hard. See you tomorrow."

After her brother left, Jen changed into her favorite purple oversized T-shirt that she liked to sleep in. She curled up in bed and stared out the window at the dark sky. Was the old Mystic Playhouse haunted?

The next week went by in a flurry of school, helping Aunt Bee around the B&B, and endless rehearsals. Mr. Hague kept the cast and crew up late every night until some parents complained, and even after that he held rehearsals till nine or ten at night.

By the following Monday, though, all the long rehearsals seemed to be paying off. When they ran through the musical from start to finish without stopping, Mr. Hague actually said, "We're getting there" at the end, instead of yelling at everyone the way he usually did.

"Have you seen the mirror Kate uses in act three?" Jen asked Stacey during a break at rehearsal that night.

"Maybe the ghooooost took it," Stacey said, her voice trembling.

Jen made a face at her best friend. "Very funny." Ever since Zeke had opened his big fat mouth last week and told everyone that she thought she'd heard a ghost in the theater, her friends had been teasing her.

"Anyway," Jen continued, "what would a ghost want with a mirror? I thought they couldn't see themselves. Not only that, but one of the trees used in the forest scenes disappeared last Wednesday, and a costume is missing, too."

"Maybe they just got misplaced," Stacey suggested.

"How does a tree get misplaced?" Jen asked, lifting one eyebrow.

Stacey grinned and shrugged.

Meanwhile, Zeke practiced a song with three other boys in the back of the auditorium. Joe Pinelli worked quietly off to the side, adding a gold braid to the edges of the carpet. Alice Pinelli had been home sick with the flu for the past week — ever since the day after the roles were posted.

"That sounded pretty good," Tom, one of the older boys, said. "Zeke, try to use more vibrato in your voice. You know, make it wobble a bit."

Zeke nodded. He'd never had formal singing lessons, but he was learning a lot working with these older, more experienced singers.

Suddenly, yells could be heard from near the stage area.

"I will not shut up!" Mrs. Kizme shouted. "I have every right to be here. My daughter is the STAR!"

The four boys groaned in unison.

"There she goes again," Tom said, rolling his eyes.

"I'm glad my mom isn't like that," another boy said.

"You are the worst director in the world," Mrs. Kizme screeched.

"Get out of here," Mr. Hague screamed back. "You are no longer allowed at my rehearsals. Get out!"

"I could direct this musical better than you!"

"Over my dead body!" Mr. Hague bellowed.

"Well then, I'll just have to see what I can do about that, won't I?" Mrs. Kizme snarled as she stalked out of the theater, pushing things and people out of her way and giving a tremendous slam to the door as she left. It seemed like the entire building shuddered from the impact.

"Sheesh," Stacey whispered in Jen's ear, where they were standing on the side of the stage. "That sounded like a threat to me."

"A death threat," Jen agreed.

Kate Kizme pushed past the girls, her hands covering her face.

Jen and Stacey looked at each other. "She looks upset," Stacey whispered.

Jen nodded and hurried in the direction the older girl had taken, thinking maybe she could comfort her. Angry voices came from the back corner of the stage, behind the painted scene of the village. Jen peered around the edge of the scenery.

Heather Elliot stood facing Kate, her hands on her hips, her feet spread wide. "You have to tell them."

Kate, her voice still choked with tears, said, "No— not yet."

Heather angrily stomped her foot. "If you won't, then I will."

"No!" Kate reached out and grabbed Heather's

arm. "Don't you dare. I *said* I'd take care of it. Now leave me alone."

Heather yanked her arm free and leaned in closer to Kate. "If you don't hurry up and do it, I'll do it for you, and then you'll be sorry! Not only that, but I'll . . ."

Jen leaned forward to hear the threat. What on earth were they arguing about? It wasn't a friendly little conversation, that was for sure.

Suddenly Heather spotted her. "What are you doing, spying on us?"

"Uh," Jen said, "not really, I just wanted to make sure Kate's okay."

Heather sneered and looked at Kate. "Oh, she's just fine. But not for long," she added under her breath as she stalked away.

Jen watched her go, then stepped closer to Kate. "Are you okay?" she asked.

"I'm fine," Kate said, rubbing her eyes.

"Do you want me to get Mr. Hague?"

Kate held up her hand to stop Jen. "I'm okay," she managed to croak. "Really. But don't tell anyone what you heard, okay?"

Jen bit her lip. Why didn't Kate want anyone to know that Heather had been threatening her?

"Promise?" Kate demanded.

"Sure, I guess so," Jen agreed, not sure this was the right thing to do.

Kate gave her a slight smile. "Thanks." With that, she walked away.

Still not sure she'd done the right thing, Jen went around the back of the stage, looking for Zeke. At least she could tell him what she'd overheard.

Mr. Hague was at the edge of the stage showing a boy where to stand. Something above the director caught her eye and she looked up, first with curiosity, then in horror. The heavy light that hung from the catwalk far above shifted as though someone were pushing it. Then, almost in slow motion, she watched the spotlight come loose and plunge toward the stage!

After Hours

"Watch out!" Jen screeched, rushing forward.

Mr. Hague swiveled to stare at her, saw her pointing finger, looked up, and jumped out of the way all in a split second. The light crashed to the wooden stage floor with a splintering of glass and a clanking of metal.

For a moment, everyone stopped what they were doing and stared in shock.

Mr. Hague came to life first. "She tried to kill me," he shouted with fury. "Mrs. Kizme tried to kill me!"

Zeke showed up at Jen's elbow. "Are you okay?" he asked.

"I'm fine," Jen said, feeling a little shaky.

"Talk about lights out," Tommy said, joining them.

Jen ignored his lame joke. "Do you think Mrs. Kizme really did try to kill him?"

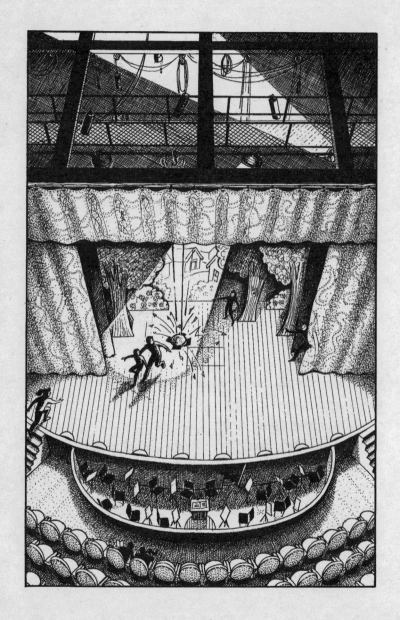

Zeke frowned. "How? She only made the threat a little while ago, on her way out of the theater. She couldn't have sneaked back in such a short time and rigged the light."

"What if she planned it ahead of time?"

"You mean loosened the bolts or something so that the light would fall?" Zeke shook his head. "Too chancy. The light could have fallen at the wrong moment and killed her own daughter."

Jen looked up at the catwalk. It was empty. Had she seen someone up there right before the accident, or had it simply been the light shifting? Or a ghostly hand?

By this time Joe Pinelli was examining the broken light fixture. Mr. Hague stomped around him. His face had been chalk-white a moment ago; now it blazed red with fury.

"I'll get her," he growled. "I'll get her for trying to kill me!"

"I think it was just an accident," Joe said, beginning to sweep up the broken glass. "One of the workmen on the catwalk must have loosened the bolts and forgotten to tighten them. Perhaps when Mrs. Kizme slammed the door, it loosened the light even more."

"See?" Mr. Hague shouted. "It was her fault! She tried to kill me!"

"It's just that this theater isn't ready for a show,"

Joe stated rather harshly. "And by the way, no one can use any of the seven bathrooms. There's a leaky pipe that needs fixing. There's a portable toilet outside if you need it."

Mr. Hague stomped his foot. "What? How can we have rehearsals if the indoor bathrooms don't work? What kind of theater is this?"

Joe narrowed his eyes at the director. "That's your problem."

Mr. Hague waved his hands in the air. "Amateurs! You're all amateurs! What am I going to do?"

Everyone was used to Mr. Hague's crazy behavior by now, and they drifted back to what they'd been doing before the crash.

"Pretty peculiar accident, if you ask me," Jen mumbled. "Mrs. Kizme threatens to kill Mr. Hague, then he almost does get killed. And not only that, but Heather was just threatening Kate, and Kate made me promise not to tell anyone. Something really strange is going on, and we have to figure out what it is."

Zeke nodded in agreement. "Be careful," he warned. She nodded, a grim look on her face. Once Jen had disappeared backstage, Zeke offered to help Joe clean up the mess.

"How's your wife?" Zeke asked the old man as he held the dustpan.

Joe cleared his throat. "Oh, she'll be fine. Just a touch of the flu, I suppose."

Zeke didn't say anything. Alice Pinelli's *touch of the flu* had lasted for a week now. He hoped it wasn't something more serious. Aunt Bee would be really upset if anything was wrong with Alice.

He helped Joe carry the bag of broken glass and bent metal pieces out to the Dumpster on the side of the building. As they stepped back into the theater, Larry Tomkins approached them.

"Mr. Pinelli," Larry said, a friendly smile on his face, "that was some accident, wasn't it?"

"Accidents happen," Joe said stiffly.

Zeke continued walking, but as soon as he heard the next words out of Larry's mouth, he paused.

"Like the accident with Alaina Shine?"

"What are you talking about?" Joe demanded.

Zeke doubled back, staying in the shadows. He, too, wanted to know what Larry was talking about.

Larry chuckled, holding his small tape recorder under Joe's chin. "Don't play innocent with me. I know it was your boat that Alaina was sailing on when she disappeared."

"You'll mind your own business," Joe threatened, "if you know what's good for you."

"Is that a threat?" Larry asked.

"Take it as you will," Joe spit out. With that, he stalked away.

Larry smiled after him and then tucked his tape recorder into his top pocket.

Zeke couldn't believe what he'd heard. Alaina Shine had been in Joe's sailboat when the storm hit? She had never been found, and neither had the boat. *Joe's boat!* What did it mean? Did Joe have something to do with Alaina's disappearance? With her death?

Zeke's mind raced as he searched the backstage area for Jen. He had to tell her what he'd overheard.

He found her surrounded by costumes, a needle and thread in one hand and a strip of Velcro in the other. He crouched down and told her about the boat. Jen's eyes widened, but she continued sewing.

"Wow," she said when he'd finished. "Poor Mr. Pinelli's had to live with that guilt all these years."

"Poor Mr. Pinelli?" Zeke repeated. "How do you know he didn't do it on purpose? Maybe he put a hole in the boat or something."

Jen bit the inside of her lip. "I don't know," she finally said. "Mr. Pinelli does seem secretive about something, but he sure doesn't seem like a murderer."

"That's how murderers get away with stuff," Zeke said ominously. "They don't seem like murderers. And not only that, but he threatened Larry."

Just then a shout came from the stage. Mr. Hague's voice blasted through the air. "Victim number three, you have two seconds to get out here!"

Zeke paled. "Oh, no, that's me!"

Jen smirked up at him. "Uh-oh, the director doesn't sound too pleased with victim number three! Can you get killed more than once?"

With a worried look, Zeke hustled away. Jen laughed to herself. Mr. Hague was full of barks, but she hadn't seen him bite anyone yet.

The rehearsal continued until 10:15. Finally, Mr. Hague sent everyone home. "Don't forget what you've learned tonight," he threatened. "The first performance is less than two weeks away!"

Zeke got ready to go. Larry had offered to drive them home so Aunt Bee wouldn't have to come out. He zipped up his windbreaker and found Jen still painting a large piece of scenery.

"Come on," he said. "Larry's ready to go."

Jen looked up, a dab of purple paint on her nose. "I can't leave yet. We're just going to stay and finish this so it'll be dry by tomorrow." She motioned to Kate, who was also painting. "Kate said her mom will give Tommy and me a ride home. Don't worry. We're almost done."

Zeke said good-bye with a shrug and headed

out to the parking lot to meet Larry. Personally, he wouldn't want to get in a car with Mrs. Kizme and have to listen to her rave about Kate the whole way home.

The theater emptied out quickly until only Jen, Kate, and Tommy were left painting the last bit of scenery. The three of them worked in silence for half an hour. Even Tommy managed to keep quiet as he concentrated on painting clouds across the otherwise blue sky.

Jen looked at Kate's portion of the scene. The older girl was painting the garden beside one of the village houses. The flowers looked real.

"You're a great painter," Jen said.

Kate smiled. "Thanks."

"Did you take lessons?"

"Nope, I just spend a lot of time sketching. Flowers are a special favorite of mine."

Jen was about to say something, but an odd rushing noise distracted her. She looked up. The sound seemed like it was coming from directly above her. Kate and Tommy heard it, too.

"What *is* that?" Kate asked, looking around her nervously.

"Sounds like waves crashing or something." Jen frowned and cocked her head. "But that's impossible."

The thunderous sound filled the empty theater and seemed to be coming from every direction. After a few moments, though, the noise began to fade and a deathly silence descended.

"What was that?" Kate asked again.

"You mean, what's that sound now?" Tommy said in a hushed voice.

Jen's skin prickled. Now that the sound of rushing water was gone, she could hear another noise. The eerie moaning was back!

A Falling Star

"That's the sound I heard last week," Jen said.

"You mean Alaina Shine's ghost?" Tommy squeaked. He started gathering the paintbrushes. "I'm out of here!"

Kate stood up and began to clean her area as well. "It is a pretty spooky sound," she said.

"Well, it looks like we're done anyway," Jen said, glancing at the scenery. "We can leave it here to dry."

"Let's get out of here," Tommy said urgently, as the strange noise rose to a higher pitch.

Without looking back, the three of them rushed out of the theater. Outside, not a single leaf fluttered in the still air.

"It definitely wasn't the wind," Jen muttered.

"Do you think that was a ghost then?" Tommy asked, just as Mrs. Kizme pulled into the driveway.

"I do," Kate said. She shuddered. "It even sounded like Alaina Shine to me. Like a ghostly version of her singing. But don't say anything to my mom. She'll freak."

Mrs. Kizme stopped the car and the three of them jumped in. None of them wanted to linger in front of the scary-looking theater so late at night.

"How was rehearsal?" Mrs. Kizme asked brightly. "I'll bet Mr. Hague missed me once I was gone."

Tommy opened his mouth to say something, but Jen kicked him softly to keep him quiet.

"So why did you have to stay late tonight?" Mrs. Kizme asked.

"Uh," Kate said, "I wanted to run through the werewolf scene using the props. Jen and Tommy were helping me out."

Jen sat quietly the rest of the way home. If Kate didn't want to tell her mother about the ghost or the fallen light, she wasn't going to break the news either. But why wouldn't she want to tell her about painting scenery? Well, it was none of her business why Kate lied to her mother. Tommy looked at Jen and shrugged, obviously coming to the same conclusion.

After a silent ride home, Jen tiptoed through the quiet B&B and went to bed. She fell asleep with the strange playhouse moaning echoing through her head.

After school the next day, Zeke hurried home to help Aunt Bee clean the rooms before rehearsal. Four more reporters had arrived to write about the show and the revived interest in the life and tragic death of Alaina Shine.

Cleaning was his and Jen's job, but he'd let Jen off the hook today so she could go check on the scenery at the theater. Even though he made a fuss, he really didn't mind cleaning the rooms, and he knew that Jen knew it. He liked order, which was why his room was neat and clean. Jen's room, on the other hand, looked like a tornado had torn through it. He grinned at the thought. Looking at their rooms, no one would guess they were twins, that was for sure!

He finished with the guest rooms on the first floor and stepped into the small lighthouse museum to give it a quick dusting. The museum occupied the first floor of the lighthouse tower and was filled with old lighthouse memorabilia and photos and documents, some that were as old as the lighthouse. Some were even from the founding of Old Mystic Village itself. He and Jen had "curated" the exhibition themselves.

"Oh," Zeke said with surprise when he pushed through the door, "I didn't think anyone was in here."

Larry turned from the cabinet of old photos he'd been inspecting. He gave Zeke a brief smile. "Just looking around," he said.

Zeke started dusting, watching Larry out of the corner of his eye. He was sure the reporter had already looked around the museum. Why was he in here again? Was the man that interested in the past?

After a few silent moments, Larry gave Zeke a wave and left. Frowning to himself, Zeke couldn't help wondering more about Larry. On a hunch, he dropped his dust cloth and ran two flights up the circular stairs to his room. He booted up his computer, logged onto the Web, and searched the *New York Times* on-line for articles by Larry Tomkins. He couldn't find anything with Tomkins's byline.

If he didn't work for the *New York Times*, where did Larry Tomkins really work? As Zeke walked back through the foyer on his way to clean the guest rooms on the second floor, he found Larry behind the front counter, looking through the guest book.

"Can I help you?" Zeke asked pointedly.

Larry grinned. "Just curious about who's stayed here. I guess it's the reporter in me."

"Really?" Zeke said. "By the way, I looked for your name under the *New York Times*, but couldn't find it. I wanted to see some of your work," he explained.

"Oh, no, I never said the *New York Times*. I said the *Newark Towns*," Larry corrected quickly. "You must have misheard me.

"If you want a ride to the theater, I'm heading over there in about half an hour," Larry went on.

"Uh, sure," Zeke said, realizing he'd have to hurry up with the cleaning if he wanted to catch a ride. "I'll be ready." He dashed up the stairs and tackled the second-floor guest rooms. The *Newark Towns*, he thought. He'd never heard of that paper, but he could have sworn Larry had said the *New York Times* when they'd first met. Zeke had excellent hearing and he rarely, if ever, misheard anything.

At any rate, he didn't have time to check it out on-line, not if he wanted a ride to rehearsal. For the next half hour he swept, dusted, and straightened, reviewing his lines in his head as he worked. He didn't want to give Mr. Hague another reason to yell at victim number three!

Jen grabbed Stacey's arm and dragged her toward the Mystic Playhouse. "You have to come with me," she begged her best friend.

Stacey's bright blue eyes widened. "Don't tell me you're afraid?"

"Not afraid," Jen said quickly, "but the moaning really was spooky. And now that Tommy and Kate heard it, too, I know I'm not imagining it."

"If it is Alaina Shine's ghost," Stacey said thoughtfully as they walked along, "I'm going to have to check it out. Maybe her ghost will tell me what happened to her forty-three years ago."

"You're nuts," Jen said, grinning at her friend. "I thought you were scared of ghosts."

"I am," Stacey admitted. "But it'll be a great addition to my article!"

"Anything for a story," Jen teased.

When they arrived at the theater, Jen paused before going in. She didn't want to admit she was a bit nervous, but she couldn't help the shiver of fear that made her hands jittery as she reached for the door handle. Telling herself she was being foolish, she gave a hard tug and walked in with firm steps. No supposed ghost was going to scare her off! She flicked on the lights at the main power panel. Stacey followed her to the area where the scenery lay on the floor.

"Oh, no," Jen cried, staring down at the smeary mess that had once been the pretty garden Kate had painted last night.

Stacey gasped. "What happened?"

Jen crouched down and touched her fingers to the ruined backdrop. "Someone dumped water on it. Who would do such a mean thing?"

"There are some buckets over there near the back wall," Stacey said. "I'll bet whoever did this used those buckets to carry the water."

"But why?"

"Obviously someone's not too happy about this musical being performed."

Jen bit her lip. Stacey was right. Just because she and Zeke and the rest of the cast and crew were excited,

didn't mean everyone was. After all, even Aunt Bee said she wished they weren't reviving *The Werewolf in the Woods*. But then again, Aunt Bee wouldn't do something like this in order to stop the performance from going forward.

The two girls cleaned up the mess. As they were finishing, others began to arrive for rehearsal. Just as Zeke and Larry got there, Mrs. Kizme charged into the theater, waving a sheaf of posters in her right hand.

"Look at this, everyone," she crowed. "I found an old poster for *The Werewolf in the Woods* in the basement with Alaina Shine's picture on it. I've updated it to promote our show."

Jen and Zeke joined the crowd gathering around Mrs. Kizme. Alaina Shine looked pretty and very young in the black-and-white poster, not at all like the glamorous star she became after she went to Hollywood. Now the poster read REVIVAL across the top, and someone had printed the new performance information along the bottom.

"I found this with a bunch of other old photos and such," Mrs. Kizme went on. "Isn't it perfect?"

"I thought she wasn't allowed in here," Stacey said under her breath.

Jen nodded. When had Mrs. Kizme snooped

around without being seen? Did she have anything to do with the things missing lately? But that didn't make sense. Why on earth would she want to sabotage a show starring her daughter? Still, the woman had obviously been sneaking around here without permission. *What was she up to?*

"Get out!" Mr. Hague suddenly shouted, pushing his way through the crowd. "I thought I told you never to set foot in this theater again!"

Mrs. Kizme bristled. "For your information, you don't own this place. Anyway, I just wanted to show everyone the posters. And," she went on, a triumphant smile curling her red lips, "I wanted to tell you that three talent scouts have confirmed seating reservations for opening night! Not only that, but television crews will be here as well."

Mr. Hague pointed at the door, his wild hair looking even more disheveled today. "Out!"

Mrs. Kizme gathered up the posters and left in a huff.

Mr. Hague glared around at the cast and crew. "I'm so glad to hear there are agents coming," he said. "I hope I'm discovered and whisked off to Broadway where I can direct *real* actors, not a bunch of amateurs who stand around gawking. Get busy!" he snapped.

Jen looked at Zeke, lifting one eyebrow. She knew

they were both thinking about how much Mr. Hague wanted to get away from Mystic. Would he do anything and everything to draw more attention to the show and possibly get "discovered"?

"Wasn't that old photo great?" Stacey asked, jabbing Jen in the ribs to get her attention. "I have to see if I can find some other old stuff for my article." She rushed off without looking back.

"Wait," Jen called after her.

A surprised cry came from the front of the stage, distracting Jen. Next came a tumbling crash, followed by a wail of pain.

Mistaken Identity

Worried that another light had fallen — and landed on someone this time — Jen joined the group that had gathered at the edge of the stage. Below them, Kate Kizme sat on the ground, clutching her ankle. Tears streamed down her cheeks.

Jen jumped off the stage and crouched next to the girl. "What happened?"

"I think I sprained my ankle. I — I fell off the stage."

Jen looked up. It was at least three feet up. Heather stood at the edge of the stage staring down at them, her arms crossed, a slight smile twisting her lips.

Jen lowered her voice as a sudden awful thought struck her. With Kate out of the way, Heather would take the leading role! "You weren't pushed, were you?"

Kate's tear-filled eyes flickered up to hers. "Uh, what do you mean?" Then her glance moved beyond

Jen to Heather. But she quickly looked away again.

Jen frowned. Had Heather pushed Kate off the stage? And was Kate hiding it for some reason?

Joe Pinelli arrived just then with a bag of ice. Kate gratefully accepted it and pressed it to her ankle. A friend of Kate's helped her into a chair, and Jen heard her say she'd called Mrs. Kizme to pick her up.

As Mr. Hague clapped his hands for order and instructed Heather to get ready to take Kate's place for this rehearsal, Jen wondered how much Heather wanted the starring role. Enough to push the other girl off the stage? Instead of just a sprain, Kate could have broken her ankle, or worse! After all, Heather had threatened the star once already.

When Mr. Hague didn't get the fast results he wanted, he began to shout, wildly throwing his hands around his head. He even kicked the air a few times. One of his air-kicks knocked over a large tote bag he carried around with him.

Jen jumped forward to help pick up the mess that had spilled out of the canvas bag. It was mostly music CDs. As she gathered them, she noted that some were modern rap music, but lots of them were recordings of old musicals and operas.

"Never mind," Mr. Hague snapped, grabbing the stack out of Jen's hands. "I'll do that. Get back to work."

"You're welcome," Jen mumbled as she climbed the steps to the stage. When she glanced back, she saw that the director had shoved all the CDs back into his bag and now he was yelling at some poor boy about not screaming enough when the werewolf attacked him.

Zeke watched Mr. Hague, telling himself he would be the best victim in the show. Maybe he'd even get a standing ovation.

The next hour of rehearsal passed uneventfully. It was almost time for Zeke's grand entrance, so he positioned himself off stage right, waiting for his cue. He looked around, waving as Tommy walked by behind him, carrying a load of fake wood for the campfire scene. Kate Kizme stood to the left, her back to Zeke.

He tapped her on the shoulder and asked, "How's your ankle, Kate?"

When the girl turned around, it wasn't Kate at all. Heather grinned at him.

"Wow," Zeke said. "From the back you looked exactly like Kate. Sorry about that."

"No problem," Heather said. She patted her shaggy wig and tweaked one of the tufted ears that stuck up. "It's this werewolf hair that fooled you. I'm taking Kate's place for this rehearsal." Then she made a face of regret. "But she should be better by tomorrow."

Zeke nodded and returned to his position to wait

for his cue, when he'd stroll onto the stage and pretend to be gathering acorns in the woods. Soon after, the werewolf would attack him and he'd die. He couldn't help grinning. The fake blood they were using would look absolutely real to the audience.

As he waited, his mind wandered back to his mistaking Heather for Kate. Heather obviously wanted the leading role. Did she want it enough to push Kate off the stage? Maybe he should warn Kate that Heather might be a hazard to her health—

"Victim number three!" Mr. Hague bellowed. "You missed your cue!"

"Rats," Zeke said under his breath. He'd blown it again. Without another thought he rushed onto the stage, prepared to die a gruesome death.

That evening, Mr. Hague ended the rehearsal early for once. Jen and Zeke were glad for a night off to catch up on their homework. They sat in the parlor, Jen reading about Mayan civilization and Zeke working on some math problems. Even Aunt Bee had settled in with them to read one of the mystery books that Detective Wilson had recommended to her.

Zeke chewed on the end of his pencil. Math was not one of his favorite subjects. In fact, he'd rather be doing anything else. Instead of looking at his homework sheet, he stared at the corner bookcase. A lending library sat on the middle shelves, and games were piled haphazardly on the bottom shelf. The upper shelves were filled with family photos and snapshots of famous people who had stayed at the B&B.

One black-and-white photo in particular caught his eye. He sat up straighter.

"Aunt Bee," he said, "is that you?" He stood up and lifted the framed photograph off the shelf.

Jen and Aunt Bee looked up.

Aunt Bee smiled. "Why yes. That was taken when I was fifteen."

Jen peered at the picture. "You kind of look like Alaina Shine did," she said. "Mrs. Kizme showed us an old poster of her."

Aunt Bee nodded. "I suppose I do, a little bit. That's because while all the other girls were waving and bobbing their hair, Alaina and I kept ours long. From the back, we practically looked like twins."

"And you still have long hair," Jen said, looking at Aunt Bee's long gray hair, which she normally kept in a braid down the middle of her back. Right now the braid dangled down over one shoulder.

"I wonder if Alaina still has long hair," Zeke mused.

"You mean her ghost, don't you?" Jen said.

"If that is her ghost, and if she's really dead," Zeke said. "But if she were alive, do you think she'd have long hair?"

Aunt Bee shrugged. "Maybe. I only know that all those years in Hollywood she did. Whenever a role called for short hair, she refused to cut it. She wore a wig instead."

Zeke returned the photo to the shelf. He stretched and yawned. "I think I'll finish my math upstairs." He grinned. "Closer to my bed."

Jen packed up her schoolbooks, too. "I'm done." They left the parlor together, heading for the light-house tower.

The next morning, Jen dashed into the parlor. Last night she'd forgotten one of her notebooks. If she didn't have it in class today she'd be dead. She found it under the chair where she'd been sitting. Glancing quickly around to make sure she hadn't left anything else, her eyes fell on the bookcase. She frowned. Something looked wrong, out of place. No . . . missing! Aunt Bee's old photo wasn't where it was supposed to be.

"What did you do with Aunt Bee's photo?" she asked Zeke as they hurried out to the parking lot.

"I didn't do anything with it," Zeke said. "You saw me put it back."

"It's not there now," Jen replied. She also told Aunt Bee as they clambered into the old station wagon.

"I'm sure it's there," Aunt Bee said. "No one would want that ancient thing. Perhaps Zeke put it back on the wrong shelf?"

"Maybe," Jen agreed, deciding she'd take a better look when she got home. But by the time the day was over and rehearsal had ended and Jen finally dragged herself up the front steps to the B&B, the last thing she wanted to do was search for an old picture. Still, something bothered her about the fact that it had been missing. She knew that no matter how tired she was, if she didn't look for it now it would bug her all night and she wouldn't be able to sleep.

She dragged Zeke into the parlor with her. "See," she said, "it's not — "

Zeke cut her off. "It's right where it's supposed to be."

Jen blinked. Yup, there it was. "But I'm sure it was missing this morning. I'm positive."

Zeke frowned. He believed Jen. She might be a little sloppy, but she had a great eye for detail — that's why she was such a good stage manager.

Jen picked up the picture and examined it more closely. "Look." She held it out to Zeke. "The picture is crooked in the mat. It wasn't like that before, was it?"

"Nope," Zeke said. "Someone must have taken it out of the frame and then replaced it crooked."

"Weird," Jen said. "Who would do that?"

"And why?" Zeke added.

The Search

Usually Jen set her clock-radio alarm for six o'clock in the morning. Thursday morning, however, she was awakened abruptly by someone banging on her bedroom door.

"What?" Jen cried grumpily. She peered at the clock through sleepy eyes. It was only five-thirty.

Zeke pushed open the door. Right away Jen knew something was terribly wrong.

"What?" she said again, only this time a nervous fear gripped her throat and she felt wide awake.

"Stacey's missing," Zeke said. "Her mom just called. Stacey didn't sleep in her bed last night. She's been gone all night."

"Oh, no!" Jen jumped out of bed. "Where is she?"

Zeke rolled his eyes. "What did I just say? She's *missing*. She's gone. No one knows where!"

"Did they call the police?"

Zeke nodded. "Hurry up and get dressed. Aunt Bee says we should help search for her."

As soon as her brother left, Jen scrambled into jeans and a sweatshirt. Her heart pounded and her mouth felt dry. Her best friend was missing!

A sudden thought occurred to her as she shoved her feet into her sneakers. *The ghost.* Stacey had said she wanted to investigate the sounds and interview the ghost if possible. Had something horrible happened to her at the haunted playhouse?

By the time she'd raced down to the kitchen to find Zeke, she was sure that's where they would find her friend.

"Come on," she shouted as she raced by, heading for the door. "I think I know where she is."

"Be sure to call us right away if you find her," Aunt Bee called after them. "I'm going to stay with Mrs. Sullivan until Stacey returns."

Jen explained her hunch to Zeke as they mounted their bikes and whizzed down the long driveway to the road that would take them into town. Dawn was just a faint orange glimmer out over the ocean.

"I hope you're right," Zeke said.

They didn't say anything else for the rest of the ride. When they got to the theater, they were both out of breath.

Jen jabbed a pointed finger at the numbers on the keypad. She'd been given the combination for the electronic lock to use for the run of the show. But when she grabbed the handle and turned it, the door wouldn't open.

"What's wrong?" Zeke asked over her shoulder.

"I must have pressed the wrong numbers." She took a deep breath and tried again. This time she heard a click as the electronic lock released. "Come on, it's open," she cried, yanking the door wide. They rushed into the theater. Jen turned on the lights, but it still looked gloomy.

Zeke grabbed her arm. "Listen," he whispered. "Do you hear anything?"

Jen stilled, cocking her head. Zeke had much better hearing than she did. She finally shook her head.

"Me neither," Zeke said. "Wouldn't Stacey be making a racket if she were trapped in here?"

Jen's mouth dried up. "Yes. Oh, no, I knew it — she's unconscious! The ghost knocked her out, or — or worse." Jen knew she sounded like a panicky idiot. Usually she could act calm, even in the worst situation. But, then again, her best friend's life had never been in danger before.

They crept quietly across the stage and searched behind every prop and piece of scenery. Nothing.

Next, they walked up and down every aisle in the audience area.

"Look at this," Jen called softly. She picked up a soft brown sweater. Lace trim adorned the cuffs and neckline.

"Someone must have left that here during rehearsal," Zeke said, glancing quickly at the sweater.

Jen shook her head doubtfully. "I don't think so. I can't see a kid wearing something like this. It looks old, but it isn't a costume, or I'd know. It says it's made of mohair and silk." Something else on the label caught her eye. She blinked. In the dim lighting she wasn't sure she'd seen correctly.

Turning the label to catch more light, she gasped. "Zeke, there are initials sewn onto the label: A. S."

"So?" Zeke said, down on his knees, peering under the seats.

"A. S. . . . Alaina Shine!"

Zeke jerked his head up so fast he knocked it on the underside of one of the seats. "Ouch! Let me see that." Rubbing his head with one hand, he took the sweater with the other.

After a close inspection, he said, "How could it belong to Alaina Shine? Who would leave this here? Her ghost?" He dropped the sweater over the back of a seat.

"I don't know," Jen said impatiently. "Never mind, let's keep looking for Stacey."

Now that the first search hadn't located even the smallest clue, Jen felt the panic rising in her chest again.

"Stacey!" she shouted impulsively. "Stacey, are you here?"

"Shhh," Zeke hissed. "Do you want to wake up the ghost?"

"But we have to find Stacey."

Zeke nodded. "You're right. STACEY!" he yelled even louder than Jen, his voice echoing like a cannon blast through the empty theater.

A dull thump came from the stage. The twins looked at each other. Stacey or the ghost?

"Stacey?" Jen called out.

Another thump answered.

Zeke ran up the steps to the stage. "It's coming from under here," he said, motioning to a heavy trunk full of costumes and shoes. "Help me move it out of the way."

Together, they shoved the trunk over. When they looked at the floor, Jen spotted the faint outline of a trapdoor. "Look!" she exclaimed, pointing. "It's so actors on stage can disappear right before the audience's eyes. Help me lift it!"

Now the thumping was even louder, coming from right below them.

Jen lifted the handle and tugged upward. Slowly the trapdoor opened.

"It's about time," Stacey said, popping her head up through the opening. "I thought you'd never get here!"

Jen was so relieved to see her best friend she practically pulled Stacey up the ladder, then gave her a big hug. Even Zeke hugged Stacey, he was so happy to see her.

"What happened?" Jen demanded, after she made sure Stacey was okay and nothing was broken or missing or sprained or bruised.

"I'm fine," Stacey insisted. "I'm not hurt at all. I came here late last night to hear the ghost. When nothing happened, I remembered Mrs. Kizme mentioning those old photos in the basement. I knew about this trapdoor and I didn't know how else to get down there. But while I was looking around under the stage, the trapdoor suddenly slammed down, and I heard a scraping sound."

"That must've been the trunk being pushed over the trapdoor," Jen explained.

"So when I tried to get out, I couldn't. I was trapped under there all night." Stacey shuddered. "I kept the light on, so it wasn't too scary. Oh, and I also found the missing props! Someone hid them in the corner under a blanket. What the heck is going on?"

Jen frowned. "I don't know, but it sure doesn't sound like a ghost doing all this."

"We'd better call Aunt Bee and your mom," Zeke said, suddenly remembering that everyone was still worried about finding Stacey.

By eight o'clock, the theater was filled with Stacey's family, the police, Detective Wilson, Aunt Bee, and Joe Pinelli.

Mrs. Sullivan hugged Jen and Zeke. "Thank you so much for finding my baby," she said, tears about to overflow.

"I'm not a baby, Mom," Stacey insisted.

Mrs. Sullivan turned to her daughter with a severe look on her face. "Just because I'm happy as pie to have you back safe and sound, that doesn't mean you won't be grounded for life for sneaking out like that, young lady!"

Jen and Zeke hid their grins. They knew Stacey would talk her way out of any serious punishment.

"We have to get to school," Zeke said, checking his watch.

"Wait a second," Jen said to him under her breath. She slipped away and looked for the sweater with the A. S. sewn into it. She wanted to take one more look at it, but it was gone. After a quick search around the area, she gave up.

With a flurry of thanks and good-byes following them out of the theater, the twins rushed off to school. Along the way, Jen told Zeke about the missing sweater.

"That's strange," Zeke said thoughtfully. "Who could have taken it in that short time?"

"I don't think it was the ghost," Jen said. "In fact, I don't think there is a ghost at all. A ghost couldn't lug a trunk over the trapdoor to lock Stacey in. Some real live person is up to something, and we have to find out what it is — and who. Already Mr. Hague and Kate have been close to getting seriously hurt, and Stacey was trapped overnight."

"The next thing that happens could be even worse," Zeke added.

"Maybe if we can figure out what that haunting sound is at night, we'll solve the mystery," Jen suggested as they pulled up to the Mystic Middle School bike stand.

Zeke nodded. "Tonight," he said solemnly. "We'll sneak in there tonight."

"I just hope we don't get trapped the way Stacey did."

That night, pale, ghostly clouds blew across the dark sky.

"I'm glad we're sure it's not a ghost haunting the old place," Jen said as they crept closer to the theater, "because tonight is the perfect night for a haunting!"

Zeke didn't say anything. He felt sure they were

dealing with a real person, too, but that didn't mean there wasn't a ghost involved, also! He decided to keep this thought to himself for now.

They'd hidden their bikes in the bushes around the corner. Now they approached the theater as quietly as possible. The side door was still unlocked. Zeke pulled it open slowly, careful not to let it squeak or bump into anything. They slipped in. The theater was dark, but no darker than it was outside.

"I don't hear anything," Jen whispered. "Do you?"

"Not yet," Zeke replied.

At that moment, a woman stepped into the very faint light given off by the night-lights that were left on when the theater was empty. The twins froze. The figure took a step forward, then paused, as though listening to something only she could hear.

"It looks like Aunt Bee," Zeke said, just barely whispering.

It did, Jen realized. Without thinking, she called, "Aunt Bee?"

Zeke grabbed her arm. The woman jerked as though startled, then fled into the shadows. Someone else's pounding footsteps came from the direction of the center aisle of the seating area.

"Run!" Zeke gasped.

10

A Perfect Match

Jen turned and caught a quick glance of the person running toward them, then she followed Zeke through the backstage area. They made it to the side door and burst through, running as fast as possible across the street and diving headfirst into a large cluster of bushes.

The man chasing them stepped through the door, but stopped there. He turned his head this way and that, then retreated, pulling the door closed firmly behind him.

"That was close," Zeke said, his heart still thumping madly in his chest. He turned to Jen and glared at her in the dark. "Why did you call out like that? If that was Aunt Bee, didn't you realize how much trouble we'd be in? Especially after what just happened to Stacey?"

"Sorry," Jen said. "I was just so surprised to see her there."

"That woman couldn't have been Aunt Bee, though," Zeke said.

"I know," Jen agreed, "or she wouldn't have run away like that. Who was it?"

"And who was the man chasing us?"

"I recognized him," Jen said quickly. "That was Detective Wilson, and he almost caught us. I just hope he didn't recognize us, too, or he'll tell Aunt Bee, and we'll be in big trouble!"

"Come on," Zeke said, scrambling out of the bushes, "let's go home. I've had enough excitement for one night."

"Fine," Jen agreed. "We'll try again tomorrow night."

"No way!" Zeke said.

The next day at school the twins could barely keep their eyes open through their classes. Fortunately, Mr. Hague made them so nervous they had no trouble staying on their feet through rehearsals. But after practice that night, Jen was still trying to convince Zeke that they needed to sneak back into the Mystic Playhouse.

"I don't think it's a good idea," Zeke protested.

"Aunt Bee said that Detective Wilson was hired to guard the playhouse because of what happened to Stacey. We can't go sneaking around behind his back."

"He won't catch us," Jen said. "We still haven't found out who's making that haunting noise. If we give up now, we'll never figure out everything that's been going wrong since rehearsals for *The Werewolf in the Woods* started."

"But what about Aunt Bee?"

"She went out somewhere. She said she'd see us tomorrow morning."

Zeke knew when Jen had him beat. "Okay," he finally agreed. "But if we don't hear anything tonight, we give up, okay? We'll find some other way of figuring out what's going on."

Jen nodded. She'd agree to anything right now, just to get Zeke out of the B&B and on their way. A little while later, they were once again sneaking in through the side door of the theater. This time they knew to expect Detective Wilson. Sure enough, there he was, sitting in a first-row seat near the stage with an open book on his lap, illuminated by a battery-operated book light.

"Is he reading?" Jen whispered in Zeke's ear.

He shrugged.

"Do you hear anything?" Jen asked.

As if on cue, the strange moaning began. It

sounded louder than the other two times Jen had heard it. Loud and spooky. *It's not a ghost*, she told herself firmly. *Not a ghost!*

"Look at Detective Wilson," Zeke whispered.

"What about him?" Jen asked. He looked the same to her.

"Doesn't he hear the sound?"

Then it hit her. Detective Wilson wasn't responding to the haunting moans at all. It was as though he couldn't hear them, but as far as she knew he wasn't going deaf. She'd never noticed him wearing a hearing aid or anything.

She didn't have time to wonder any further. Zeke tugged her hand and led her toward the sound, which, luckily, was away from Detective Wilson. When they reached the rear of the seating area, they stopped and listened intently.

"Sounds like it's coming from upstairs," Zeke said.

"This way." Now Jen led the way into the lobby and up the stairs to the balcony area. A door marked PRIVATE led up to the third floor. The sound seemed like it was coming from up there.

Trying to tiptoe, they mounted the final flight of stairs. Jen pulled out the tiny microcassette recorder she'd brought and flicked it on, holding it out in front of her like a candle.

At the top of the stairs, they paused. Jen could barely see Zeke in the extremely dim light, but she could tell what he was thinking. The odd, haunting sound they'd thought was moaning wasn't moaning at all. It was singing!

They were now so close to the sound, Jen was even afraid to whisper. Instead, she mouthed the words, "Let's see where it's coming from."

Zeke nodded to show he understood.

Together, they crept forward. The first door on the right stood slightly ajar. Jen peeked in. From the glow of the streetlight coming in through the window, she saw what looked like a practice room, with an upright piano against one wall and a music stand set up in the middle of the room. No singer in there. The next door also stood open. A small bathroom. Empty.

The singing was closer now. Just two more steps. . . . That's when Zeke kicked something hidden in the shadows. It clanged and clunked loudly. The singing abruptly stopped.

They knew that Detective Wilson would soon come running. Feeling a bit of déjà vu, the twins scrambled down the third-floor stairs. They waited until they heard Detective Wilson charging up one set of stairs from the lobby, then they took the other stairs down to the main floor.

Without looking back, they ran along the side aisle, up onto the stage, and over to the Cast and Crew door. They didn't stop running till they'd retrieved their bikes. They jumped on. Even then they didn't slow down, but pedaled furiously through the dark streets and out of town toward the B&B, which stood blinking brightly on the bluff overlooking Mystic Bay.

"That was way too close," Zeke gasped as they chugged up their long driveway.

"It sure was, but at least we have that singing on tape!" Jen said as a glimmer of light behind them caught her eye. She turned and recognized the odd tilt to the front headlights on Aunt Bee's old station wagon. "Oh, no," she exclaimed. "Aunt Bee's coming home now!"

They both knew if they didn't make it inside before their aunt caught a glimpse of them, they'd be in big trouble.

"Hurry up," Zeke panted, pedaling harder than he'd ever pedaled before. It felt like his legs were on fire.

Jen huffed and puffed behind him. They finally made it to the top of the steep driveway, sped to where they parked their bikes, skidded to a stop, jumped off, and raced around back and through the kitchen door.

Zeke laughed between gasps for breath. "Man,

that was way too close, too!"

Jen couldn't help the nervous giggles that escaped her. Adventure was one thing, but being home safe and sound wasn't so bad, either.

"Hello, you two," said a voice behind them.

The twins whirled around.

Larry smiled at them. "What are you up to?"

"Uh," Jen said, "we were just running around the yard. You know, we had extra energy we wanted to work off before going to bed."

Larry made a point of looking at his watch. "Oh, I see." He didn't sound like he believed them.

At that moment, Aunt Bee strolled into the kitchen. "My goodness," she exclaimed. "I didn't expect to find anyone up."

"I'm just helping myself to some tea," Larry said quickly. "You did say that was all right, didn't you?"

"Heavens yes," Aunt Bee said, throwing up her hands. "Do you need any help?"

"No, no," Larry said. He looked at the twins. "Jen and Zeke were helping me. Everything's fine."

Zeke smiled thankfully at the reporter, though it did irk him a bit to be in his debt. Why, he had no idea.

"Then I'm off to bed," Aunt Bee said. She yawned.

"And my tea is done," Larry said, picking up his

mug and following her out of the kitchen. "Good night, you two," he said over his shoulder.

The twins listened to their footsteps fade away and breathed a sigh of relief. Jen removed the cassette player from her pocket, where she'd stashed it as they'd run away from the theater. She hit rewind, and the two of them listened to the whirr of the tape without saying anything. When it was finished rewinding, Jen pressed the play button.

At first the eerie singing sounded muffled, like the moaning Jen and others had heard on previous nights. But as they moved closer to the source of the singing, the voice became clearer and clearer. In the background, very, very softly, violins and flutes could be heard accompanying the voice.

Zeke tipped his head, listening intently. "You know," he said slowly, "that person sounds familiar."

"Really?"

"Hang on, I'll be right back." He rushed out of the kitchen and returned a couple minutes later, lugging the portable CD player. He plugged it in and with a grin said, "Listen to this."

Jen couldn't believe it as the first selection wafted out of the small speakers. It was the same voice. Not only that, but she knew exactly who that voice belonged to!

11

What's Next?

"I don't believe it," Jen exclaimed. "That's a CD of one of Alaina Shine's original recordings, isn't it?"

Zeke nodded triumphantly. "Someone's been playing her old music in the playhouse for some reason."

"Maybe that someone wants people to think the Mystic Playhouse is haunted," Jen suggested.

"Then why play the music on the third floor where no one can hear it very well? Onstage it just sounds like a moaning ghost."

"Right," Jen agreed. "You'd think the person would want everyone to know the place was haunted by Alaina Shine and make it more obvious."

Zeke tipped his head to the side, listening to the music. "To scare people away?"

"Or to get them even more interested in the performance. The Pinellis would make more money if more people came to the show," Jen pointed out. Then she frowned. "On the other hand, they aren't too thrilled about this musical. Maybe they were trying to scare people away?"

"Or it could be Mrs. Kizme or Mr. Hague," Zeke said thoughtfully. "The more excitement over this revival, the better. It'll draw even greater attention if the playhouse is haunted. You know, more agents, more press. Or how about Kate? She doesn't seem very happy to have the leading role. Maybe she's trying to scare people away from the show."

Jen shrugged. "But that still doesn't answer the question of why someone would play the music on the third floor where it can hardly be heard. I mean—"

Zeke put a finger to his lips, interrupting her. "Did you hear that?" he whispered.

Jen shook her head. All she could hear was Alaina Shine's voice drifting softly out of the speakers.

Zeke tiptoed to the door of the kitchen and poked his head out, looking toward the front lobby. Jen followed, trying to step as quietly as possible. They stealthily made their way into the front foyer. Zeke then peeked into the parlor.

"Oh," he said in his normal tone of voice, "it's just Woofer and Slinky. I thought I heard something."

With that mystery solved, the twins returned to the kitchen and turned off the CD.

"You know," Jen said thoughtfully, "I think I've seen a CD of Alaina Shine's music recently." She frowned. "If only I could remember when and where."

"Maybe tomorrow we can search the third floor of the playhouse and find a clue," Zeke said.

The twins passed through the dining room and climbed up the lighthouse tower stairs. Zeke said good night to Jen at her door and climbed up one more circular flight to his room. He didn't bother turning on a light but changed quickly into his pajamas and slipped into bed. Just as his eyes drooped closed, he remembered that he'd left the CD player and the tape recorder in the kitchen. He was tempted to just leave it till morning, but he didn't want someone to walk off with their tape. It could be evidence.

He hurried back to the kitchen and grabbed the CD player, then he looked around for the small tape player. The black microcassette recorder was nowhere to be found. Zeke looked under the table and on the chairs, finally deciding that Jen must have grabbed it before they'd gone upstairs.

Three minutes later, Zeke was back in bed. After such a tiring day, it didn't take him long to fall asleep.

~⌄~

The next morning, Zeke arrived in the kitchen just after Jen. Aunt Bee stood at the stove frying eggs and bacon. Blueberry scones were baking in the oven and made his mouth water.

He sat down next to Jen and said softly, "Don't lose that tape."

Jen looked at him with one eyebrow raised. "What tape?"

Zeke rolled his eyes. "The one from last night."

"I don't have it," Jen said slowly. "Don't you?"

Zeke quickly explained how he'd come back down last night but found the tape recorder missing.

Jen's heart sank. Without that tape, they had no proof that the eerie moaning was really Alaina Shine singing. They *had* to get that tape back.

"Aunt Bee," Zeke said in a casual tone, "did you see Jen's tiny tape recorder down here this morning?"

Aunt Bee turned from the stove with a platter in her hand. "No, did you misplace it?" She placed the food on the table, then opened the oven and removed the steaming scones. "Do you want me to ask the guests if anyone saw it?"

Jen and Zeke looked at each other.

"Never mind," Zeke said quickly, "I'm sure it'll turn up."

As soon as they'd finished eating and it was time to get ready for rehearsal, Jen said to Zeke in an undertone, "Someone must have taken it. It didn't just walk out of here on its own."

"Maybe one of the reporters picked it up, thinking it belonged to them," Zeke suggested.

"In the middle of the night?" Jen said doubtfully.

Zeke shrugged. "Do you have a better suggestion?"

"Then we'll have to ask them when we see them."

Zeke nodded in agreement. As soon as Larry walked into the lobby to drive them to rehearsal, Zeke asked the reporter if he'd mistakenly picked up Jen's recorder.

Larry shook his head. "You left it in the kitchen? Are you sure it didn't fall on the floor?"

"We're sure," Jen said as they walked out to Larry's car.

"I'll keep my eyes open," Larry offered. "And I'll ask around for you, too."

The hustle and bustle of rehearsal wiped all thoughts of the missing tape recorder from Zeke's mind. He had to practice a song for a couple of hours, then some of the other victims asked how he died so well, so he took the time to coach them on writhing in pain.

Backstage, he saw Heather in the werewolf wig again. He called after her, but she didn't seem to hear him. "Heather!" he called louder. This time the girl stopped and turned around, but it wasn't Heather at all.

"Oh, hi, Kate," Zeke said. "I thought you were

Heather because you don't have your crutches." He grinned sheepishly. "My mistake."

Kate gave him a thin smile. "No problem," she said, then she slowly limped away.

Zeke watched with narrowed eyes. Had she been limping like that a second ago? He really couldn't remember, but he didn't think so. Maybe he just hadn't noticed because he'd been assuming it was Heather, since Kate wasn't using her crutches. Whatever. He had more important things to think about. And one of them was yelling at him right now.

"Victim number three!" Mr. Hague bellowed. "You've missed your cue again!"

Zeke groaned as he ran onstage. Maybe he wasn't cut out to be a victim after all.

By Sunday morning, the tape recorder hadn't turned up, even though they had questioned each reporter and even some of the other guests.

Jen sighed as she opened the *Mystic Village Beacon* Sunday edition. Suddenly, an article headline caught her eye. "Listen to this," she said, after she'd scanned it. She began to read aloud. " 'Revived Musical Hottest Thing in Town. As everyone knows, *The Werewolf in the Woods* will be performed at the old

Mystic Playhouse on Friday night, the exact fiftieth anniversary of Alaina Shine's rise to fame, fortune, and tragedy.'" The article went on to detail Alaina's background and her mysterious disappearance.

"This is the interesting part," Jen said. "'Many out-of-town reporters are covering the story and have already descended upon our small town. Not only is the old story of Alaina Shine sparking new interest all over the country, but rumors abound that the Mystic Playhouse is haunted. Some even say it's being visited by Alaina Shine's ghost. "I'm sure the theater is haunted," comments Larry Tomkins, theater critic. "And on opening night I'll have some stunning news to deliver about Alaina Shine and the haunted playhouse!" When asked for further information, Mr. Tomkins simply gave a secretive smile and said, "Let's just say I'm not so sure it's a ghost doing the haunting!" and then refused to answer any more questions. Personally, this reporter can't wait until opening night. Will Alaina Shine's ghost show up for the performance?'"

Jen looked up from the paper. "I wonder what he's talking about."

"*We* know it's not a ghost haunting the playhouse," Zeke said. "But what does Larry know that we don't?"

12

Knocked Out!

At Thursday's dress rehearsal, the excitement and nervousness about Friday's opening night performance had reached a fever pitch. Knowing that there would be so much coverage of the show had put everyone on edge. Everyone, Jen realized, except Kate and Heather.

"What are those two up to?" she whispered to Zeke during a break in the rehearsal.

Zeke turned to look at the older girls. They stood partially behind one of the side stage curtains, giggling about something.

"I thought Heather hated Kate for getting the lead role," Zeke said.

"I did, too," Jen said. "But they're acting like they're best friends or something."

"Didn't you say that you thought Heather pushed Kate off the stage the other day?" Zeke asked.

Jen nodded thoughtfully. "It sure seemed like it."

"I think something fishy is going on," Zeke said.

"Me too." She looked at her brother and knew without asking him what he was thinking. Jen grinned. "Let's go, bro!"

Smiling back at her, Zeke headed toward Kate and Heather, who stopped laughing and whispering as the twins approached.

Zeke cleared his throat. Keeping his voice low so as not to be overheard, he said, "Uh, Jen and I noticed something weird going on with you two. First, Heather seemed like she was totally jealous of you, Kate, but now it's like you're best friends."

Kate and Heather glanced at each other quickly.

"We might as well tell them," Kate said to her friend. "I heard they're good at figuring out stuff, and we don't want them telling anyone else, right?"

Heather shrugged and tucked a piece of her blond hair behind her ear. "Fine with me." She looked at the twins, narrowing her eyes. "But you two have to promise not to breathe a word about this to anyone!"

"We promise," Jen said quickly. *What on earth is going on?* she wondered.

"Well," Kate said slowly. "I really don't like to perform. I was just born with a great voice, but I'd rather paint scenery and make costumes. It's—it's my mom who pushes me. Uh, you've probably noticed."

"You're not kidding," Zeke said.

Jen jabbed him with her elbow. Luckily he got the hint and stopped talking. Jen could tell it would only make Kate feel worse.

"So anyway," Heather continued with the story, "since I love to perform, Kate offered to let me have the part. But we had to be tricky about it because Mr. Hague and Mrs. Kizme would have a fit if they knew what we're planning."

"So you really didn't fall off the stage?" Jen asked.

Kate shook her head, her long dark hair waving back and forth. "Nope."

"Aha," Zeke said with sudden understanding. "That's why you weren't limping the other day."

"Right," Kate said. "I'm not such a great actress after all. The *accident* was just to give Heather a chance to practice the part onstage with the others."

"But how are you going to get out of performing on opening night?" Zeke asked.

Kate grinned. "Don't worry, we have a plan."

"Remember," Heather warned, looking a bit worried, "you promised not to tell anyone."

"Don't you think you should talk to your mom about this, since you hate it so much?" Jen said to Kate.

Kate looked at her feet. "Yeah, I know." She looked up again. "And I will . . . right after the performance. I promise. If I tell her now, she'll freak."

Mr. Hague clapped his hands at that moment. "Let's go," he shouted. "Back to work!"

Right away everyone bustled into action. Jen hurried over to the director. She had to have the werewolf's tail approved, since Mr. Hague hadn't liked any of the previous models. This one had a wire in it to make it look like it was waving back and forth when it was worn.

"That's much better," Mr. Hague said, nodding.

Jen couldn't help feeling a glow of pride, since the wire had been her idea.

Mr. Hague turned abruptly to yell at one of the actors, knocking over the large bag that always seemed to be at his side. Jen automatically stooped down to help gather the scattered CDs. Her heart jumped. This was where she had seen the Alaina Shine CD! Sure enough, she picked one up. Just as she was examining it to see if it was the same one they had at home, Mr. Hague pulled it out of her hands.

"Get back to work," he said brusquely.

Jen didn't even mind his rudeness this time, and she ran off to find Zeke.

"Wow," said Zeke after she'd told him what had happened. "So maybe he's the one playing the music on the third floor of the playhouse."

Jen nodded eagerly. "Could he think all the attention from Alaina Shine's ghost will make it easier for him to get a job on Broadway in New York City?"

"I wonder if he's the one who locked Stacey in the basement," Zeke said.

Jen frowned at that thought. It was one thing to pretend to be a ghost, but it was another to practically kidnap her best friend. "We'll have to keep an eye on him so he doesn't do something even more drastic."

They didn't get any more time to talk, since it was almost time for Zeke's entrance. He was determined not to miss it.

By the end of the night, everyone was exhausted. Even Mr. Hague, usually so full of energy, looked rather slumped over when he said, "Pretty good job."

"Pretty good?" Zeke muttered. "It was great."

"Then why do you look so bummed?" Stacey demanded.

Zeke sighed. "Everyone knows that when dress rehearsal goes so well, it's bad luck for opening night."

Jen tried to think of something encouraging to say, but for some reason a sense of dread filled her, too. Not that she believed in superstition, but it was as though a sense of doom hung over the playhouse. She shook her shoulders, trying to brush away the feeling.

The heavy mood didn't lift all the way home, even though Larry tried hard to cheer them up.

"Just wait till you hear what I have to say tomorrow night," the reporter said as he drove them back to the B&B. "It's a real doozy. It'll blow everyone away." He chuckled. "Mystic will be back on the map and I, Larry Tomkins, will be more famous than you can believe!"

Jen didn't feel like begging for hints, and neither did Zeke. Pretty soon Larry quieted down and dropped them off at the B&B before heading back to town to meet some other reporters for a late-night snack at a local pub.

"I can't believe I still have homework to do," Zeke grumbled.

"Me too," Jen said. "Come on, we can do it in the parlor and keep each other awake."

They settled at a small table guests used for game playing. Zeke pulled his math book out of his backpack, and Jen started on a short English essay. Aunt Bee stopped in once or twice to make sure they hadn't fallen asleep sitting up, and Woofer and Slinky eventually made themselves comfortable on the small throw rug near the couch.

When the phone rang, Jen barely noticed. She only had one more paragraph and then she'd be able to go to bed! Suddenly, Aunt Bee rushed into the room, her face pale, her hands squeezed together.

Jen looked up. "What's wrong?" she exclaimed, jumping to her feet.

"Detective Wilson's been hurt!" Aunt Bee said.

"Is he in the hospital?" Zeke asked.

Aunt Bee shook her head. "No. He was hit over the head, but he insists he's okay. Joe Pinelli is driving him over here so I can keep an eye on him in case he has a concussion."

Jen's heart raced. "This happened at the theater?"

Aunt Bee, too choked up to speak, only nodded. The twins waited with her on the front porch. Their aunt had grown very close to Detective Wilson over the last year, and they could see how upset she was.

Soon afterward, Joe swung up to the door and helped the injured man out of his car.

"Let me know if you need anything," Joe said. He prepared to leave. "I'm really, really sorry about this."

Detective Wilson winced. "Don't worry about it. It certainly wasn't your fault. You didn't do it, did you?" Then he chuckled, but Jen could see that it hurt his head to do so.

Joe left and Aunt Bee helped Detective Wilson onto the couch in the parlor. After he was settled, Zeke asked, "What happened?"

The retired detective rubbed his forehead. "I'm not really sure. One minute I was sitting there in my seat by the stage, and the next, *Pow!* The blow must have knocked me out."

"Did you see who did this to you?" Jen asked.

Detective Wilson shook his head. "I didn't even hear anything. Not a single thing."

Jen frowned. It looked like they wouldn't find any clues to this attack. Could Mr. Hague have sneaked back into the theater to play the haunting music? But why play it so late when the only one around to hear it was Detective Wilson? Or did Joe Pinelli make the attack? He had been apologizing quite a lot. Did that mean anything? Who else could have done it?

"Jen, Zeke, it's time for you to go to bed," Aunt Bee said, still fussing with the cushion under Detective Wilson's head.

Neither Jen nor Zeke protested. In fact, after telling Detective Wilson they hoped he'd feel better by morning, they hurried off, even though sleep was now the furthest thing from their minds.

They didn't stop to talk until they reached Jen's room. Without even asking, Jen withdrew some paper from her supply and tossed Zeke a pen. She knew the only way to get to the bottom of this mystery was to fill out suspect sheets.

"Exactly what I was thinking," Zeke said, beginning to write. *Who is haunting the playhouse?*

Mystic Lighthouse

Suspect Sheet

Name: Mrs. Kizme

Motive: She will do anything to make Kate famous. Would she get rid of the director so she could direct the show and make her daughter more prominent?

Clues: She threatened to kill Mr. Hague, and as soon as she left, he was almost killed in a freak accident. Accident? Or murder attempt?

She was obviously snooping around to have found the old posters of Alaina Shine . . . could she have gone back for more of the old memorabilia and found Stacey there and locked her in the basement so she wouldn't get caught?

Did she rig the "ghostly occurrences" (singing, missing props, Mr. Hague's accident) to attract attention to the show for her daughter's sake?

Mystic Lighthouse

Suspect Sheet

Name: Larry Tomkins

Motive: DOES HE WANT TO BE THE ONE TO MAKE THE SCOOP OF THE CENTURY? WOULD HE DO ANYTHING TO BE A STAR REPORTER?

Clues: WHY IS HE SNOOPING AROUND THE B&B? WHAT INTEREST COULD HE HAVE IN THE B&B?

IF HE'S SNOOPING AROUND THE B&B, COULD HE HAVE BEEN THE ONE TO TAKE THE PHOTO AND THE TAPE? BUT WHY?

Could he have arranged for the "ghostly occurrences" to get attention for the play so that his news coverage would be even bigger?

WHAT IS HIS EXTRAORDINARY SECRET THAT HE'S GOING TO UNVEIL ON OPENING NIGHT?

Mystic Lighthouse

Suspect Sheet

Name: Mr. Hague

Motive: Maybe he really does want an agent to "discover" him so he can leave Mystic. But why would he do anything to jeopardize the show by causing accidents if that were the case?

Clues: Is his temper for real or is he a kook? Or maybe he's using his crazy behavior as a way to draw attention away from his motives?

Could he have rigged the "ghostly occurrences" to bring more attention to the show for his own sake? After all, he owns some of Alaina Shine's CDs.

Mystic Lighthouse

Suspect Sheet

Name: Alice and Joe Pinelli

Motive: THEY WERE SO AGAINST THE IDEA OF REVIVING <u>THE WEREWOLF IN THE WOODS.</u> WHY?

Clues: WHY WOULDN'T THEY WANT THE ATTENTION FOR THE MYSTIC PLAYHOUSE?

EVEN THOUGH THEY WERE AGAINST IT, THEY DIDN'T DO ANYTHING ABOUT IT . . . OR DID THEY?

Maybe they used the "ghostly occurrences" to try to scare people away and get the show shut down.

Joe blamed the lights going out on the old wiring, but the wiring had recently been redone.

ALAINA SHINE WAS LOST AT SEA IN <u>JOE'S</u> BOAT. DOES HE HAVE SOMETHING TO HIDE?

Jen frowned as she reviewed the sheets. "Well," she said at last, "at least Kate and Heather aren't suspects anymore."

Zeke sighed. "That doesn't seem to be any help right now, does it?"

"Nope," Jen agreed, placing the completed suspect sheets on her desk. "Not at all."

Note to Reader

Have you figured out who is responsible for the playhouse ghost? Jen and Zeke have made pretty good notes on the suspects, but they did miss a few important clues. Without those clues, it's almost impossible to figure out what is going on.

Have you come to a conclusion? Take your time. Carefully review your suspect sheets. Fill in any details Jen and Zeke missed. When you think you have a solution, read the last chapter to find out if Jen and Zeke can put all the pieces together to solve *The Mystery of the Haunted Playhouse*.

Good luck!

Solution
Another
Mystery Solved

On Friday, right after school, Jen and Zeke rushed to the Mystic Playhouse. They had a few hours before the doors would open to the public, but all of a sudden it seemed like there were a million and two things to do before then.

Mr. Hague roared and bellowed even more than usual, and no one could keep Mrs. Kizme out.

"I have every right to be here with my daughter," she insisted. "I will not leave!"

Finally Mr. Hague gave up.

"I wonder if he's sorry he cast Kate as the lead," Stacey whispered to Jen.

Jen shrugged. She was still wondering how Kate was going to get out of performing tonight. As far as Jen knew, everyone still thought Kate was the star.

In the mad rush, Zeke caught a glimpse of Joe and Alice Pinelli. Joe was dressed in a blue suit, obviously ready for tonight's performance. Alice, looking rather pale from her long bout with the flu, wore a dark green dress with a sweater draped over her shoulders. In fact, Zeke realized, squinting in an attempt to see better, it looked a lot like the sweater Jen had found in the theater the other night, but he couldn't be positive. He waved and the older couple waved back, though they didn't smile.

At last, the crazy mad rush slowed almost to a snail's pace. To Jen, it felt like the calm before the storm. Very soon the audience would start trickling in.

Mr. Hague appeared backstage and clapped his hands for attention. When everyone had gathered around, he cleared his throat. "I know I'm a difficult director — " A soft chuckle rippled through the group. "I demand the very best." He paused. "But I am happy and proud to say . . ." Again he had to clear his throat. "You all have risen above my expectations. Tonight's performance will outshine even Alaina Shine's performance fifty years ago. I couldn't ask for a better group of actors and crew. Thank you."

For a stunned moment, there was only silence. Then a big cheer erupted and everyone clapped loudly.

Jen nudged her brother's shoulder as they continued to clap and watch Mr. Hague. "Maybe he doesn't want to go to Broadway after all. He really seems to like working here."

"Unless it's all an act," Zeke said.

Jen shook her head. "I don't think so. He really seemed sincere."

"I still think we should keep an eye on him," Zeke said as the clapping died down and everyone started to disperse.

"Speaking of which," Jen said, motioning with her head. "Look who's talking to him now."

Zeke looked. Mr. Hague had his head bent forward toward Kate as though he were trying to hear her better. Suddenly, his face turned red.

"What?" he shouted. "What do you mean you have laryngitis?"

Everyone gasped. Jen and Zeke looked at each other, and Jen lifted her eyebrow. *So this is the plan,* she mouthed.

It took a good fifteen minutes for Kate to convince Mr. Hague and her distraught mother that she really had no voice and that Heather would have to take over her role.

"I thought Mrs. Kizme was going to have a heart attack," Stacey said with a giggle a little while later. "Serves her right for being so bossy."

Although Jen agreed, a small part of her also felt sorry for Mrs. Kizme. She was sure Kate's mother only wanted what she thought Kate wanted. They would have to have a long talk very soon.

Once they opened the front doors, the excitement backstage started to rise again. Mr. Hague, who had combed his hair earlier, once again looked like a madman, with his black hair sticking straight out from his head at odd angles. Kate sat in a corner with a glass of salt water her mother kept insisting she gargle, while Heather hurried to put on her costume and makeup.

At last they got the cue that the audience was seated and the curtain would open in five minutes.

"Why wait five minutes?" Tommy asked Zeke, glancing at his watch. "It's seven o'clock right now."

Tommy's question was answered by a voice addressing the audience in front of the curtain.

"My name is Larry Tomkins, and the esteemed director has given me permission to make a short announcement before the musical begins."

Jen and Zeke peeked around the side of the curtain. They were dying to know what huge secret Larry was going to uncover.

Larry rubbed his hands together and said, "I have uncovered information about Alaina Shine and her supposed disappearance at sea."

"Supposed?" Zeke repeated.

"Alaina Shine," Larry went on, taking a dramatic pause, "is alive and well and living in Mystic, Maine!"

A gasp erupted from the audience. Whispers, sounding like blowing leaves, rippled through the room.

A reporter sitting in the audience stood up and demanded, "What are you talking about, Tomkins?"

Larry grinned. "I'm getting to that, McNeal. I've done quite a bit of investigating since I've been in Mystic. And I have proof — positive proof — that Alaina Shine is really Bee Dale, the owner of the Mystic Lighthouse Bed and Breakfast!"

The audience roared to life. Aunt Bee, who sat in the front row with the recovered Detective Wilson and the Pinellis, looked stunned. Her jaw dropped open and she looked first at Alice and Joe, then at Detective Wilson.

"What's going on?" Zeke said. He stepped in front of the curtain to stand beside Larry. Jen followed.

Larry grinned at the twins. "The proof is in this photo." With a flourish, he unrolled a huge enlargement of the photograph of Aunt Bee from the parlor. "Note the hairstyle, which was the same as Alaina Shine's." He bent down to turn on a boom box he'd carried onto the stage. "And I have a tape recording of her singing from just the other night."

Everyone listened intently as he played the tape.

"That's our recording," Jen hissed in Zeke's ear. "He stole it!"

Then Larry played one of Alaina's CDs, pointing out the similar voice modulations. There was no doubt that the voice was the same.

Another reporter stood up and barked, "Where did you get that recording?"

Larry tugged at his collar without looking at the twins and said, "I took it in this very theater!"

More gasps of amazement. Cameras flashed brilliantly as all the reporters present took notes on this extraordinary, press-stopping story. Solving this mystery would be the biggest story of the century!

Aunt Bee suddenly stood up. "Ridiculous," she exclaimed. "I'm not Alaina Shine, and it's easily proven if you took the time to ask anyone in town. I finished high school here, unlike Alaina, and I went to a local college. Then I worked at the Mystic Library until I retired several years ago. I assure you, I did not have time for a Hollywood career."

The audience chuckled.

"But — but what about the photo?" Larry stammered. "I got it from your parlor. You looked just like Alaina Shine."

"Only because we had the same hairstyle and were close friends," Bee pointed out.

"The singing then," Larry said desperately. "You were away from the B&B every night that singing was heard in the theater."

Aunt Bee smiled thinly. "I was volunteering at

the library, helping with their inventory. I do it every year. It's a long, hard job that can only be done at night after the library closes. Besides, I can't sing to save my life." She opened her mouth and belted out a few notes. They sounded awful.

By now, the soft chuckles had grown to loud laughs.

"Boo!" someone in the audience jeered. "Start the real show! Enough with the clown onstage!"

Jen felt a little sorry for Larry, but how could he have made such a huge error? Then another thought hit her, but before she could demand an answer from the reporter, Joe was ushering Larry and the twins off the stage. He led them to his private office. A moment later, Alice, Detective Wilson, and Aunt Bee joined them. Other reporters desperately wanted in, but Joe firmly shut the door in their faces.

Jen started right in on her question. "Were you the one who locked Stacey in the basement?"

Larry shifted his feet. "Uh . . ."

"You did!" Jen exclaimed, rightly guessing from the guilty look on his face.

Detective Wilson stepped forward. "That's a criminal offense," he said sternly. "You'll be lucky if you're not charged with kidnapping."

"And you hit him over the head last night," Zeke

added, motioning to Detective Wilson.

Instead of looking sorry now, Larry turned surly. "He was in the way. I wanted to catch Alaina singing and take a picture of her, but this guy got in the way. I had to take care of him."

Jen shivered. Larry now sounded more like a gangster than any kind of a reporter.

"That's why I couldn't find your name under the *New York Times*. And I'll bet there's no such paper as the *Newark Towns*," Zeke said.

"That's right, nosy," Larry snarled. "I'm a freelance journalist, and my career is down the tubes if I don't come up with a killer article. This would have made me a millionaire." He glared at Aunt Bee. "I was so sure you were Alaina Shine."

Aunt Bee shrugged. "Sorry to disappoint you, but I've never even been to California, never mind Hollywood."

Detective Wilson gripped Larry's arm. "You're coming with me to the police station. You've got a lot of explaining to do." A moment later, the door closed behind the two men.

"That explains a lot of what's been going on," Zeke said. "But not everything."

"Right," Jen continued, as if she had been the one talking. "Now we know who fiddled with Aunt Bee's photo in the parlor and who . . ." She stopped mid-sentence, realizing it would be better to leave out the late-night tape recording session. "Uh, who was sneaking around the B&B. It must have been Larry in his silent shoes."

"So it wasn't Mr. Hague," Zeke said. "He wasn't trying to fake the ghost for more attention so he could get to Broadway. I think he really likes it here."

"And it wasn't Mrs. Kizme, because she would never do anything to hurt Kate's chances at stardom. Though I do wonder about the light that almost crushed Mr. Hague," Jen added.

Joe held up his hand. "That was a real accident. When the new catwalk was installed, that light was not attached properly."

Zeke looked at Aunt Bee with a smile. "For a second there, I thought Larry was right about you."

"Me too," Jen said slowly. "Larry was close to the truth, though, wasn't he?" She looked around the small room. "Alaina Shine *is* alive and well and living in Mystic, after all." She turned to the Pinellis. "Mrs. Pinelli, your real name is Alaina, isn't it?"

Alice bit her lip, then glanced over at Aunt Bee, who gently nodded. Alice sighed and said, "Oh, dear. I knew I couldn't keep it a secret forever, but however did you guess?"

"You weren't happy about the revival of *The Werewolf in the Woods*," Zeke said, "because you didn't want attention drawn to finding the missing star. You wanted to live your life in peace without the Hollywood hassle."

Alice nodded. "Go on."

"And Zeke overheard that it was Joe's boat you were sailing on when you disappeared," Jen said. "Joe was helping you because he loved you. You must have run off together to get married, and you changed your name from Alaina Shine to Alice Pinelli. The police never found a sign of your body or of the boat because you hadn't really drowned."

"We did actually sink the boat a little later," Joe said quietly, "in case someone were to recognize it docked farther up the coast. We felt the safest thing to do would be to get rid of it."

Alice shook her head in wonderment. "You children are amazing to have figured this out."

"The sweater helped, too," Jen pointed out. "We found it that morning we came to look for Stacey. It was on one of the seats, but when we went back for it, it was gone."

"I must have picked it up and brought it to my office," Joe said. "But how did that help you figure out that Alice is really Alaina?"

"Jen saw the initials sewn onto the label," Zeke said.

Alice pulled the sweater off her shoulders and peered at the label. "A. S." she said softly. "Alaina Shine. I never thought to check that when I went about changing my identity," she added with a gentle laugh. "You two certainly are good detectives."

"One thing I don't understand," Jen said, "is the singing from the third floor."

"Even though I hated being in the limelight, I still love to sing," Alice said. "I go up there to sing to my heart's content. Usually I try to go up there when the theater is empty, but during these past weeks people came back in and thought they heard a ghost. But it was only me."

"If that was you singing," Jen said, still confused, "then how did we tape . . . I mean, how did Larry tape you singing with an orchestra in the background? You didn't have an orchestra up there with you, did you?"

Alice laughed. "Heavens no. I simply played a tape of the musical score and sang along with that." Her smile faded. "Now I suppose you'll want to tell everyone all about it? Tell them who I really am?"

Jen looked at Zeke. She knew what he was thinking. They both shook their heads.

"No," Zeke said. "We won't tell anyone."

"You've worked very hard for your privacy," Jen

added. "Your secret is safe with us."

Aunt Bee patted the twins on the shoulders and murmured, "Thata-way!"

Alice's eyes flooded with tears. "Oh, thank you so much. I have to admit I was desperate to stop the show. It was unbearable to think that, just when I thought it was finally safe to return to Mystic, this would start all over again." She looked embarrassed. "In fact, I even tried to stop the performance by shutting off the lights at the first rehearsal."

"And you hid some props, didn't you?" Jen asked.

Alice nodded. "I'm so ashamed of myself."

"Don't worry about it," Zeke said quickly. "In your situation, we'd probably do the same thing."

"Did you also dump water on the scenery?" Jen asked, remembering the ruined flowers Kate had painted.

Alice's cheeks turned red. "That truly was an accident, but yes, it was my fault." She looked at Joe, and he held back a laugh. "I, uh, used the bathroom on the third floor. I simply forgot that there was a leaky pipe. I'm very sorry about your scenery."

Jen laughed. "I don't think I'll tell anyone about that."

Zeke wrinkled his nose in agreement. "We won't tell anyone anything."

Alice smiled gratefully at the twins. "Thank you so much. The only ones who know our secret are you two, your aunt, and Detective Wilson. And I'm confident none of you, my fine friends, will betray me."

"Hey," Zeke said with a grin. "That's a line from this musical."

Not wanting to be late for the show, Joe urged Alice and Aunt Bee back to their seats. For the first time in weeks, Joe and Alice looked happy.

As the twins headed to the backstage area, Jen said, "That explains a couple other things, too, like how I thought we saw Aunt Bee here late the other night. It was really Alice, I mean Alaina, I mean Alice." She grinned. "I hope I don't give away the secret by accident!"

"You won't," Zeke assured her. "Besides, after the fool Larry made of himself, no one would believe you anyway."

In front of the curtain, the audience clapped as Mr. Hague made his way to the director's podium.

"Yikes, the show's about to start," Jen yelped, "and I have to open the curtain!"

"And I have to sing in the opening number!"

"Break a leg!" Jen called softly after him as he hurried off to get into position.

Zeke glanced back and groaned. "Don't even say that! *Good show* is good enough!"

Mystic Lighthouse

Suspect Sheet

Name:

Motive:

Clues:

**Join Jen and Zeke
in these other exciting
Mystic Lighthouse Mysteries!**

The Mystery of
Dead Man's Curve

The Mystery of
the Dark Lighthouse

The Mystery of
the Bad Luck Curse

The Mystery of
the Missing Tiger

The Mystery of
the Phantom Ship